The Parson of Gunbarrel Basin

G·K
Hall
&Co.

Also published in Large Print from G.K. Hall by Nelson Nye:

Born to Trouble
Gunman, Gunman
The Lonely Grass
Mule Man
Trail of Lost Skulls
Trigger Talks
Wide Loop
Wild Horse Shorty
Horse Thieves
Red Sombrero
Riders by Night
Wolf Trap

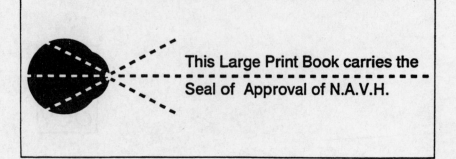

This Large Print Book carries the Seal of Approval of N.A.V.H.

The Parson of Gunbarrel Basin

Nelson Nye

G.K. Hall & Co.
Thorndike, Maine

Published in Large Print by arrangement with Golden West
Literary Agency.

G.K. Hall Large Print Book Series.

Printed on acid free paper in Great Britain.

The text of this Large Print edition is unabridged.
Other aspects of the book may vary from the original
edition.

Set in 16 Pt. Plantin.

Library of Congress Cataloging-in-Publication Data

Nye, Nelson C. (Nelson Coral), 1907–
  The parson of Gunbarrel Basin / by Nelson Nye.
    p.   cm. (alk. paper : lg. print)
  ISBN 0-8161-5923-8
  1. Large type books.   I. Title.
[PS3527.Y33P37   1994]   93–43546
813'.54—dc20   CIP

CHAPTER ONE

'Damn country's crowding up,' growled Fick, disparagingly considering across one shoulder the clutter of houses starkly framed in blue twilight as the sun dropped behind the west rim's black scarps.

Some might have found that an astonishing statement had they been staring, as Fick was, at the league on league of mustard-colored land fading northward into the valley's far reaches with nothing man-made about it but this pitiful huddle of sand-scoured adobes. Southward the desert—remindful of rusting bull-tongue ploughs—stretched into an equally blue and undisturbed infinity.

'We put a crimp in that once,' the man with Fick remembered. 'I see nothin' to stop us from repeatin' the dose.'

'The times,' Fick said dryly, 'are not in tune with violence.'

He was a middle-aged man with the smell of horses and cattle about him. His heavy black beard, thinly sprinkled with grey, was cut on the pattern of General Lee's. 'These people,' he lectured in the pedantic tones of a scholar, 'aren't weedbenders. That old man, anyway, has had all the advantages of wealth and position—'

1

'That old man,' Bates McCartrey said contemptuously, 'is trash!'

Purdon Fick's blue-veined hand pushed irascibly against the trapped heat which had collected beneath the station's wooden overhang. The same hand, lifting higher, got an engraved silver case from the inside pocket of the brown herringbone coat he always wore regardless of weather. He removed an expensive cigar from the case, glance traveling over his range boss in silence. He was not accustomed to being talked back to and it showed in the way he bit the end from the weed.

'Trash he may be, but don't mistake him for a fool. If you do you're headed for trouble.'

McCartrey, who was big enough to have broken Fick in two with his hands, scuffed the ground with the heel of a benchmade boot and, breathing deeply, turned his face away, rummaging the town with his angry eyes. He said, when he'd got a good hold on his voice, 'You've sounded him out. What did he say the last time you talked to him?'

'Said he was satisfied right where he was.'

'You should have offered him more.'

'I offered him twice what the place would bring. We'll simply have to cut down. You better move all the she-stuff back into the hills. Comb out all the old stuff right on

2

down to—'

'We can do better'n that.'

Fick looked at him, waiting.

'Four sections of grass just layin' there wastin'.'

'I pointed that out,' Fick said carefully. 'Matter of fact, I even offered to lease—'

'He's got no more right to that grass than you have. It's all open range.'

'Not around those springs.'

McCartrey waved that away. 'Four sections,' he said doggedly, 'and not runnin' enough to graze down one.'

Fick rolled the cigar across his teeth and lighted it, his narrowed glance studying the other man's features. Deep-eyed from want of sleep and with a three days' stubble darkening the jowls of his mustached face, the range boss looked exactly what he was, an overbearing roughneck, granite-minded and caring nothing for anything which stood in his way. He was the kind of man who went with big outfits, the kind that made big outfits bigger. 'You're suggesting we move in?' Fick asked.

'Figure he could stop us?'

'Probably not,' Fick admitted, 'but it would look pretty raw.'

McCartrey, grinning, said, 'You worry too much.' Dragging a hand across his forehead he waggled it at the agent, who'd stepped out with some luggage and now was perspiringly

3

trundling it across the splintery planks for one of the stages to pick up. McCartrey looked at his watch. Already the westbound was forty minutes late. 'Company,' he said, 'will have to do better'n this.'

The agent mopped his face. 'Been havin' a sight of rain east of Tucson. Three String said when he come through it looked like they was in for a cloudburst. They was usin' boats in Lordsburg yesterday.'

He went back inside, and Fick, who was resident manager for the Santa Cruz Land & Cattle Company, said to his burly-shouldered range boss, 'You better forget about moving on to Crescent. We'll find some other way—'

'What other way?' Bates McCartrey said bluntly. 'How long do you reckon that soft job of yours will last if we start shippin' out cows the way the market is now? Them bigwigs back in Chicago ain't worryin' about your girl's education. All they care about is how much profit you put into their pockets.'

This was Fick's nightmare. He stood in no doubt as to the reactions of his employers. They didn't have to live in this country or face the things he had fallen heir to over the forcible eviction of those damnfool hoemen. Nothing had been proved, but a lot of people were more than half convinced that a thorough investigation would put

4

responsibility on Straddlebug, which was what most folks called the syndicate holdings.

McCartrey said, 'You can show a profit if we take over that grass.'

Fick took a turn along the planks, his anger climbing. Frustration goaded him. He resented being boxed this way by the pressure of circumstances beyond his control—even God, it seemed, had joined the conspiracy. If only they could get some of that water, he thought bitterly, that was making lakes of the flats around Lordsburg! He had always wanted to be the kind of man his neighbors would be proud to know and fraternize with. Instead he was the object of their darkest suspicions.

He came back to McCartrey trailing tatters of smoke. 'By God, we've got to be careful,' he growled. 'The stink ain't died down over that other mess yet.' When McCartrey said nothing to that, Fick asked grudgingly, 'How are you proposing to go about this?'

The range boss grinned. 'We'll send a couple of the boys over to homestead that place. Soon's they've filed, nice and legal, you can fix up lease papers and we'll move in.'

A kind of nausea swept through Fick. His clamorous thoughts whirled like spooked horses struggling blindly to escape.

5

McCartrey's plan plugged every gap. There'd be talk, of course—there was always talk, and now there would be a hell's spate of it; but, legally, Fick and Straddlebug would be completely in the clear.

Crescent couldn't fight them, couldn't even cope with the pair who would do the actual filing. Crescent hadn't any riders or any friends who would take up for it with Straddlebug cattle on that grass. Going to court wouldn't help them—not even if they could scrape up the price to get there, which they couldn't. As McCartrey had said, the land didn't belong to them; all Crescent had under patent was the six hundred and forty acres covering the source of its water.

Certainly Straddlebug couldn't be held responsible for the actions of two men who had been severed from its payroll. They could lease their grass to anyone they cared to. And the cattle, Fick thought bitterly, wouldn't recognize anything so abstract as patents. When they got to feeling thirsty they would head for the nearest water. Crescent, before this business was over, would be glad to sell out for whatever they could get.

McCartrey's plan was foolproof.

Fick's cigar had gone tasteless and he pitched it away. He kept seeing the faces of the people around here, hearing their whispers and cringing inside him. He would never live this down—never. And then he thought of Polly. After all, goddamn it, was he that old fool's keeper? A man owed something to his motherless daughter!

As though he had found a wall against which to make his stand, he went over the thing again in his mind, fretting and pawing at the plan like a woman, shifting his weight from one leg to the other. Yet even with the resentments born of frustration gnawing him, and the knowledge of what being fired would mean in terms of his daughter's welfare, he had to swallow several times before he finally got the words out.

'What?' McCartrey seemed to have trouble hearing him.

'I said "Watch your step,"' Fick repeated.

'That mean go ahead or leave Crescent alone?'

'Goddamn it,' Fick snarled, 'do I have to spell it out for you? Do what you have to do and don't yap about it!'

The glint in McCartrey's eyes changed subtly. It wasn't exactly contempt which crept through, but it might just as well have been, Fick thought, suddenly hating him. It had been the same way that other time, McCartrey suggesting the means and the manner but not lifting a finger until Fick gave the order.

Sweat seeped through the pores of Fick's skin. He got another cigar and clamped teeth into it to keep them from clattering. He

7

showed the range boss his back and glared around at the town through the deepening shadows, afraid to strike a match lest it shake in his fingers.

'Here she comes,' McCartrey said; and Fick heard the sounds and, reluctantly turning, saw the dust boiling up from its wheels like smoke from the roofs of burning homesteader shacks.

He tried to pull himself together, knowing he'd got to do this right and feeling suddenly like a very old horse that, having run all its wind out, begins to falter. He'd got to get hold of himself, and quickly. Polly's eyes were sharp and she'd be turning him inside out with her questions if he left a loose edge for her mind to get hold of.

The stage now was rocking along past the Emporium with the bakeshop, Schenck's barber's pole, O'Dowd's Pool Hall and the dust-fogged bulk of the O.K. Feed & Livery behind it. As always, Bud Hotchkiss, the Butterfield driver, was bringing them in like a four-alarm fire. A six-horse pull and, just to satisfy his vanity, the numbskull was running their hoofs off. Headstrong as a mule and impossible to reason with as Fardel! As the damned dirt farmers Bates McCartrey had run out of here!

Fick watched the man swerve almost onto the planks in front of Beaupre's saloon, half obscuring the place with dust and flung gravel, make a wide careening swing and with his full weight on the brake, pulling hard, fetch them into a shuddering stop alongside the station overhang.

'Red Post!' Hotchkiss bawled as the guard, grabbing the mail pouch, went down over the side. 'Twenty-five minutes. You kin git hot grub right acrost the street.'

He stood up and unwrapped the lines from his hands and Fick's glance, intolerantly leaving him, went nervously to the opening door of the coach. A fat drummer in a pair of thin and tight checked trousers was backing ponderously out with grunting enough for a penful of hogs. He had to do considerable maneuvering to get his quarterhorse rear through the confines of the door's narrow dimensions. He made it, though the lintel scraped the derby hat from his head and deposited it like a dropped egg on the floor, from the dust of which it bounced to the ground, where it teetered for a moment before wobbling drunkenly under the coach.

'What's the matter?' Hotchkiss said, coming down over the wheel.

'My hat!' the fat man pointed.

Hotchkiss, bending, looked and straightened. 'Sure enough goner, ain't it?' he grinned, and, yelling for the stock tender, went on inside, wiping the grime from his face with his neckerchief.

9

The drummer, red-faced, stood helplessly swearing.

A second man stepped out of the coach in a flat-crowned hat and a black frock coat; about five foot nine and robustly built, the way Fick saw him, looking past him for Polly. McCartrey noticed other things, not having his mind divided as Fick's was. McCartrey's stare caught the moody, monolithic look of his face, the broad brawler's shoulders with the coat tight-stretched across them, as twisting, the fellow said curtly, 'Watch that talk, man,' before turning back to help the girl to the ground.

'Gambler,' McCartrey said in Fick's ear.

The Straddlebug manager looked again, gustily snorting. 'Don't you know a preacher when you see one!'

CHAPTER TWO

Bert Irish, though it did not show, was about as ill-tempered as he permitted himself to get. It had seemed a simple thing when he'd struck out so brash from Ehrenburg to keep shoving south-east and make fools of the lot of them. But the country had deceived him, placing mountains where they shouldn't be and wastelands where he had looked for

10

rolling prairies. He hadn't gone hungry—the brush abounded in wild things; but, divorced four days and three nights from civilization, it began to seem possible he'd never get out of this.

South and east the land stretched green and flat as a billiard table, but the green was the color of greasewood. There wasn't a tree or blade of grass anywhere. Nothing but sand and sun-parched adobe and cactus, of course, and this everlasting greasewood clean into the blue of those yonder mountains. The horse was beginning to show its rough usage. Irish took grim note of its plodding gait, the listless ears, the indifference displayed by that down-hang of head.

He tugged his hat lower against the pitiless glare. Might have been more sensible, he told himself now, to have crossed the river and gone into California.

Noon came and passed and Irish tightened his belt without stopping. Since daylight he had been on these flats and he knew the horse couldn't take much more of it.

He caught up his canteen again, shaking it, smiling tightly. He got out of the saddle and walked for a while. This did not noticeably improve his outlook. He presently removed his hat and poured the last of the water into it. The horse, after he'd got it, licked pathetically at the wet spot. Irish abandoned

11

the empty canteen. Then he pulled off the saddle and threw that away too.

Even thus lightened the animal's gait continued erratic. It wasn't a case of resting the gelding; its need was for feed and more water. It hadn't eaten since the middle of yesterday. Since they'd moved out of that last batch of mountains.

Irish lifted a hand to elongate the shade from his hat brim. His look found nothing encouraging. The horse had quit sweating. Irish's mouth tightened.

The horse at the end of the next hour was floundering. With a sigh Irish fetched out his pistol and shot it.

He pressed on afoot towards the wavering horizon that blurredly glimmered in the sun dance. The mountains seemed to march with him, to pace him step by tiring step. The soles of his feet burned, and, looking back, he was astonished to discover his tracks were as rambling as those left by the horse. In simple justice he ought now to shoot himself.

He considered his shadow. Night wouldn't fall for another couple of hours. It had never previously occurred to him it could get so hot in the middle of May, but he had never before been in this country—this part of it, that is. It didn't seem likely he'd ever cross it again.

He stumbled on. When he pulled up his

12

head for another burning look the mountains didn't seem to have got any nearer. His thoughts began to wander. They conjured Critchton's face and Irish swore bitterly. But for Critchton he wouldn't have been in this fix. He'd known the man had it in for him. He shouldn't have shot that fool. He shouldn't have sat in on the game in the first place.

It was Critchton who'd decided him—the stern-wheeler's captain—backing Lowe's play to the extent of a thousand dollars. Critchton had made his unfriendliness felt from the moment Irish stepped aboard. The captain had friends at Yuma; one of them had been in the game that night when Irish had broken the bank at the Bella Union. The fellow had been a part owner and Critchton had plainly been out to get back.

Irish had known this would be a grudge game but had figured he could handle anything they shoved at him. He'd watched the captain and Lowe, and the trouble, when it developed, had come from another quarter. From a man who hadn't even been in the game.

Irish had observed this fellow standing back of Lowe. After considering him awhile without discovering any signals he had not been concerned to find the man standing back of the rancher or, later, behind Colonel Cropton of the Inspector-General's

13

Department (aboard on a tour of duty). The ruddy-faced colonel, after several polite hints, had told the fellow testily to get the hell away from him. The man had moved along to stop a few hands between Irish and Critchton.

There was an unusually large pot building up on the table, and the captain, who was dealing, had been waiting for the rancher to say how many he wanted when this eye-baller drifted back to have another look at Lowe's prospects. Lowe, at that time, had been in the process of discarding.

The rancher knocked. Lowe called for a pair. The colonel took one, Irish two. Critchton dropped out of the game.

Irish, picking up his two cards, slipped them into his hand without inspection. He was keeping his eyes on Critchton and Lowe. No one had made any real killings yet.

Lowe, who had parlayed his original loan into a sizeable barricade of chips, now shoved half of these into the pot, the roof having been lifted from the game two hands before. 'Two thousand,' Lowe said, grinning. 'Going to cost you gents real dough to see this.'

Cropton, peering around with a sigh, pushed his cards face down into the discard. 'I guess that shuts out the cavalry.'

Irish matched Lowe's smile.

The draw had given him a queen and the

14

final eight. Four eights in straight poker, the way the hands had been running, looked safe as the Bank of England. 'Your two thousand,' he said, coolly moving four stacks, 'and I'll raise to whatever you've got left in that pile.'

Except for the sounds from the steam-driven engine and the water cascading from the stern-wheeler's paddles the cabin became suddenly uncomfortably still.

Lowe's eyes turned opaque and commenced to tighten around the edges. He rubbed his nose and finally shrugged. 'All right. I'll have to count 'em.'

While he was doing so Critchton lit a cigar. The colonel looked with envy at the stakes and set his glass down. Irish knew the game thus far had been completely on the level. He watched Lowe and Critchton closely. The rancher pitched in his cards. 'This is over my head.'

'Twenty-three hundred,' Lowe glowered, pushing his pile in. 'Let's see what you've got.'

Irish put in the chips to meet it. 'Four eights,' he said, and turned over his cards.

Lowe's cheeks with their crinkling burnsides turned grey. His right hand fisted above the place where his cards lay, his left hand clutching the table edge, white-knuckled. In that moment of stillness with Irish narrowly watching him the man back of

15

Lowe stepped around, declaring flatly, 'You've got a crook at work here, gentlemen. That eight of clubs came out of Lowe's discard.'

At once every man at that table was on his feet, kicked-back chairs striking the wall, one toppling over.

Irish said, tight-lipped, 'How about that, Lowe?'

Lowe's eyes, in the lamplight, gleamed like black opals. Sweat put a sheen on cheeks the color of putty but he managed a frightened nod. He said, voice thickening with blustering belligerence, 'I sure as hell threw an eight of clubs away!'

It suddenly came to Irish who this man beside Lowe was—this fellow whose lie had been designed perhaps partly to distract him but mainly for its probable effect when retold at an inquest over Irish's dead body. The man was Ben Bristol, long rumored to be another of the Bella Union's part owners.

Irish had no time then to connect with the rest of it; his contained reaction to the challenge was something they hadn't looked for. With a desperate oath Bristol snatched out a gun and, from the corners of his eyes, Irish saw Critchton reaching. Irish shot.

Flame in the lamps rushed bluely up their chimneys. Even as the light was snuffed by the concussion he saw Bristol, twisting, stagger and collapse. He saw the rancher's scared eyes and Critchton's grin stretching wickedly, then all was black, a shouting confusion of moving shapes crisscrossed by pistol fire.

His hand found the door. He flung it open, dropping swiftly, and heard the rush of unseen bullets flying into the night's whimpering blackness. He balanced his chances with his gambler's cool mind and, bending double, dived through the opening.

He ran up the deck past dark cabin windows, stripping out of his coat, remembering to fling it overboard and sailing his hat fiercely after it. The hour was too late for strollers, but this uproar, he knew, would soon have the whole boat aroused. When he guessed he was far enough forward to clear the paddles he pulled off his boots and jumped.

The chill of the water took his breath away. He was not a good swimmer, but gave it everything he had, knowing if current or suction dragged him into the paddles he was done for. He could feel the pull like hands clawing at him and fought desperately.

Somewhere behind him Lowe was crazily shouting: 'Critchton—Critchton!' and the captain's furious: 'Where the hell is he?'

'In the river!' someone yelled. Another voice cried, 'Over there—look towards the bank! About ten foot out from the shore, below that alder.'

Pistols barked like angry dogs. Bullets striking the water made Irish's arms work more frantically. His knee hit something rough and ungiving. Terror rushed into his mind. He went under.

When he came up, farther down, coughing, half strangled from the water he'd swallowed, he was out of the current, could see the black shoreline. Muzzle lights were still winking with their cork-stopper popping, but the boat was too distant for eyes to pick him out now. His feet touched bottom. He floundered out of the river and lay panting, exhausted.

But he dared not remain there. Ehrenburg was too near. Critchton would alert the authorities and the hunt would be on. By morning the region would be swarming with posses.

Irish got to his feet and set off up-river.

He had not realized how near the town was. Within a quarter of a mile, cresting a low ridge, he saw its lights. Critchton's boat was blowing for a landing.

The flat blankness of the surrounding night pressed in on him, sharpening Irish's mounting sense of despair. Here and there lone pinpricks of light from unseen dwellings accentuated the blackness and gave to the stars the brilliant semblance of crushed jewels. Close at hand then Irish discovered the deeper black of buildings and broke towards them at a shambling run.

Pain from the scraped knee made itself manifest. As he came into the yard a dog commenced yammering and he called to it, cursing it under the wheeze of his breathing when his attempts to make friends only heightened its racket. He caught the skreak of a door and a voice called gruffly, 'What's goin' on there?'

The dog's clamor subsided to a series of low growls. Irish made out a man's shape behind the dull glint of gun steel. 'I fell off that damn boat.'

'Git the lamp lit, Sary. We'll hev a look at this feller.'

Irish, eyeing the dog, wisely stayed in his tracks. Light came through a window. The man with the rifle said, 'Step over here.'

Irish limped forward. When the butter-yellow shaft from the lamp struck across him the dog circled closer, barked again and stood bristling. 'So you fell off the boat,' the man said. 'Aim to catch it?'

'If you can loan me a horse.'

'I ain't makin' no loans at this time o' night.'

'I've got money.' Irish shivered as the cold soaked through his clothing. 'Willing to pay anything reasonable,' he scowled, thinking back to what he'd left aboard the packet. 'Buy a nag if I have to.'

The man grinned. 'Over this way.' He

disappeared in blackness.

Irish limped after him, unable to still his teeth. His feet felt as though he'd been tramping through stubble. They came into a stable and the man lit a lantern. Irish swore when he heard the man's price and saw the horse. The fellow, watching his face, said, 'You can walk if you want to.'

'This all you've got?'

'I can do better. But not for that money.'

'Do it,' Irish said, and when he saw the blazed-faced sorrel he nodded. He was watching the dog when the man jostled against him, pressing back out of the wind. 'You'll want a saddle, blanket an' bridle...'

'And a water bag.' Irish knew the man wasn't fooled. Fellow had probably heard the shooting. 'I could use a hat, too. Shoes and coat if you've got them.'

'I got this old army-issue canteen,' the man said, holding it out to him. 'You want a gun to go with that harness you're wearin'?'

Irish's hand touched the leather. He managed another nod. 'Watch him, Trig,' the fellow said, and vanished again, moving off into the night.

Irish looked at the dog, more greatly upset than he'd have cared to admit. Without a gun he felt naked. It went deeper than that. He felt like Samson shorn of his hair. Shivering uncontrollably he moved out of the light.

He filled the canteen at a rainwater barrel, the dog staying with him, grimly watchful as a hawk. Irish got the gelding ready for travel and wedged a rummaging hand inside his wet shirt, not touching the gold but extracting a sheaf of damp bank-notes, conscious of the bristling stare of the dog. He distributed this currency among the pockets of his trousers to get around any show which might provoke additional danger. Watching the dog's gleaming teeth he cursed Bristol and Critchton to a fiery hereafter. The dog was a big brute. Probably enjoy a taste of gambler, Irish thought, adding up his chances.

The man returned, carrying coat, shoes and hat. Irish lost no time getting into them. His teeth quit chattering when he got the coat buttoned. It fitted better than the shoes did. The man, smiling faintly, produced a six-shooter from the waistband of his frazzled-looking trousers. 'Call it an even five hundred,' he said, handing the weapon to Irish, butt forward. 'Payable as of now.'

Irish stared at him sharply. 'You related to the James boys?'

For all that Irish stood with the gun pointed at him the man gave no sign of backing down from his demand. He shook his head at the dog. He said, 'That gun ain't loaded.' Then he held out a box of cartridges, grinning.

'Lucky for me you don't play poker,' Irish grunted. He tipped the gun's barrel and went stiff with shock. It was a .45 calibre in a .44 frame. The barrel had been cut down and there was no thumb prong on its hammer. It was the gun with which he had shot Ben Bristol.

*　　*　　*

Even now, three nights and four days later, he still felt cold fingers every time he recalled the slickness of the way that fellow had disarmed him. He'd supposed, when the man had first called his attention to the emptiness of his holster, he had lost the gun getting away from the boat. He understood now it had been when the man had jostled him. It was a frightening knowledge, undermining all his confidence.

He took the pistol out now, replacing the spent shell he had used on the horse. He shoved it back in its leather, dropping the box of cartridges into his coat pocket. Twisting his head he looked back but could no longer see the saddle he'd abandoned or even the sorrel, but the glimmer of the discarded canteen still mocked him.

He suddenly stiffened. Any motionless metal object reflecting the sun should have created a glint, a constant pinpoint of motionless light. What he actually saw was a

22

flickering, a series of uneven flashes, not motionless but pacing him.

This, Irish reminded himself, was the way panic started. A kind of madness of imagining, like thinking you saw water where there could not possibly be any.

Turning around, moving on, a croaking gasp of scornful laughter tore from the burning dryness of his crack-lipped mouth. Now he was seeing the water, too! Water in the midst of this waste of sand and rock!

He shook his head to clear his gaze and still the water glimmered. He cursed the Judas sight for the mirage he knew it was. Cursed the winding thing behind him and the weedbender's shoes that were still too big for his swollen feet. And staggered on, determined not to be taken in either by the illusion of fancied pursuit or this preposterous lake which was bound to retreat no matter how fast he went hurrying towards it, unapproachable as the Mexican border he must reach if he would escape the law.

He lost track of time. The lake still glimmered, cool and wicked as a dead man's hate. Beyond it were buildings laid up of unplastered adobe—he could even see the shadows of the *vigas* across their fronts and the group of heads-down cattle browsing the green of the farther shore.

Irish's eyes, pulling away, picked up a haze

of dust that showed against low hills to the west of the lake. He even stopped to stare at this while he sleeved his streaming face. The dust was moving, coming nearer, and he cursed it, too.

He clawed out of the coat and threw it away from him. The night would be cold, but what difference? Unless he hoarded his strength he would never feel it. Then he remembered the boxed cartridges and floundered back to recover them. Some weights a man had to pack regardless. Like the weight of the gold in his money-belt. And the pistol.

He rasped a hand across the stubble that roughened his cheeks and with his throat dry as cotton squinted again towards the lake. He saw a girl come around the far corner of the ranch house and again stared, breathless with the look of her ethereal beauty. Then the dust from the hills cut across the mirage, distorting the vision, obscuring it.

Irish, seething with outrage, shook his fist at the dust and became aware it was real. He spun around for the coat and snatched it up, frantically waving it. Horses were boiling out of that dust, the beat of their hoofs a kind of a *obbligato* to the rattle and clank of a swaying coach.

* * *

24

The stage fetched Irish to Gila Bend.

It was dark when he got there. Being Saturday till daylight the Reata—a honkytonk favored by the cow crowd—was still in full blast, despite the lateness of the hour, when he limped down the length of its crowded bar for a drink and a few guarded words with the owner.

The man's stare ran over him sceptically. 'Maybe,' he said, and jerked a thumb at the balcony. 'Try the third door,' he grunted, turning away to speak with a customer.

Irish climbed the stairs and curled his lip at the room. He pushed shut the door and propped a chair under the latch. Taking the pot from the commode he dropped the dwindling weight of his money-belt into it and wearily shoved the thing under the bed. Without striking a light he shrugged out of the coat and fell full length across the bed, exhausted.

He awoke to a ravenous hunger. His mouth held the taste of having chewed through a hog trough. He got up stiffly, aching all over.

A fist was pounding the door. Irish toed away the chair and a man came in with a plate of eggs and bacon and a jug of steaming coffee. There was a tape around his neck and he said he would take Irish's measure and have the clothes ready in time for the night's play.

25

'By ten?' Irish asked, and the fellow snorted.

'If they're not ready by seven they won't ever be. I'm pulling out on the eight-thirty stage for Palo Verde. I'll bring you a shirt when I come up with the rest of it.'

That was all right with Irish. He guessed the man would be some surprised to discover his latest customer riding the same coach.

Irish certainly aimed to be on it. The Palo Verde stage would connect with other lines running north to Prescott and north by east to Globe. By dropping off at Apache Junction he could fade with a horse into the desolate Superstitions. They'd have the devil's own time tracking him through those peaks and canyons. In the guise of a mustanger he could pick up a coach westbound from El Paso, and south of Tucson he could hole up if need be in one of those obscure off-trail towns until things were right to slip over the border.

If he seemed to be taking the long way round he had reason. Ben Bristol had been the husband of the Governor's only daughter.

CHAPTER THREE

Four days later, a few minutes short of noon, Irish disembarked from an Abbot-Downing coach in front of Tucson's turreted stage station. Packing his saddle he struck out up Main, a black-whiskered ruffian with a brawler's shoulders, clothed in the brush-clawed garb of a mustanger and, moreover, smelling like one, a fact of which he was well aware.

He started to turn in at Levin's, but a more careful inspection of the plug-hatted gentry standing around in the shade of its side-street gallery decided him against it. He tramped on, finally going into the Palace on Meyer where he signed for a room under the name of Clark Moulton.

It was while he was on Pearl, seeking hard cash for a number of bank-notes, that he saw the sign Mountain Oysters on the surprisingly clean window of an across-the-street hash house. This was a working-man's part of the town where his own rough appearance was unlikely to attract notice. Having been on scanty rations for the last several days he cut over, and stepping inside the narrow length of the place was just in time to behold a customer departing from the otherwise solidly patronised counter.

27

The little restaurant was packed, and Irish, intent on gaining the seat before someone else got it, would normally have noticed the shabby man brushing past him. Perhaps it was the white oleander in the departer's rusty cutaway that twisted Irish's head about. He found the other man's face in the pale and startled process of executing the same maneuver.

Grey eyes stared into widening black ones. For a breathless second both men hung motionless, then the fellow in the cutaway scampered for the doorhole like a terrified mouse.

The man was Lowe. And Lowe, Irish knew bitterly, would be haring off now in a hunt for the nearest law.

Someone else had dropped onto the stool he'd been after, but Irish wasn't thinking about stools any longer. Pushing through the milling stablehands and teamsters he rounded the counter and got into the kitchen. A blast of heat surrounded him with the mingled smells of cooking food. He saw the cook, in soiled white, look around from the oven. A sallow-cheeked helper, catching up a big rolling-pin, was coming round the table when Irish, growling unintelligibly, slammed through the back screen and got into fresh air.

He found himself in a fenced yard given over to refuse and a conglomerate assortment of broken boxes, bottles and rusting tins. Dropping over the fence he crossed a dusty lot. A frowsty cur reared up from a clutter of rubbish and commenced a half-hearted barking as Irish ducked into a narrow covered passage bisecting a row of foul-smelling shacks. Irish paused there a moment, knowing he could not afford to let himself be stampeded.

It was tough luck running into that fellow, but if he used his head he might yet win clear. They would obviously alert all the feed lots and liveries. They'd put on a watch on the roads, but there'd be some confusion. There were eight thousand people around this town, and, of them all, only Lowe could make identification positive.

First thing, then, was to change his appearance. Above all, he must not act like a fugitive. He moved unhurriedly into the street, ignoring the flies and the stench of rotting garbage. The dog had gone back to scratching itself, but now a child was squalling, and raised and abusive voices came through the screenless door of the house next ahead and to the left of him. There was the sound of flesh striking flesh. The kid yelled again and then Irish was past and a redheaded slattern in a torn black petticoat came running after him with a sniveling and naked little girl in her arms.

'Mister—' the redhead called, 'hey,

mister!'

It always irritated the hell out of Irish to have other people attempt to foist their problems on to him, and right now, with trouble of his own, it made him furious. But because he was, under the hard ungiving look he showed the world, essentially kind and with a strong, inherent (although frequently repudiated) sense of responsibility, he turned and irascibly waited.

'If you don't mind,' the woman smiled nervously. 'I'd admire to walk a little ways with you.' She pushed the sun-streaked hair back out of her eyes and hitched the little girl around to where her weight came against the off-side of an ample hip. 'When Tim gets to drinkin' there just ain't no livin' with him.'

An angry-looking bruise was discoloring her left cheek. She seemed younger, a lot more comely, than Irish had imagined. He kicked a rotten orange out of his way. She had almost to run to keep up with him. What she probably needed was a bruise on the other side.

She pushed the hair back again and her eyes, like a child's, openly rummaged his face. 'I expect you think I'm terrible bold, but—'

She broke off in alarm, clutching the child closer to her, as heavy brogans threw up an approaching clatter behind them. Irish, scowling, spun around to confront a glowering bullwhacker.

The man was big and his look was ugly. He'd been drinking all right and he was one of those brutes who should never have started. He was beginning to shake out the coiled whip in his fist and there was nothing Irish could do but hit first.

He sprang, piling into the man, crowding him against the rough side of a building, whacking him across the face with his pistol. Blood ran, the man staggered, the woman and the child in her arms started screaming.

Doors banged. The woman dropped the child and tore into Irish with the fury of a tigress. The man, through a spate of outraged cursing, yelled, 'Hang on to 'im, Nell! Hang hold of the whiskered divil till I git this—'

Irish bolted.

*　　*　　*

When the stage left Pearl and Pennington at five after three in the afternoon, Irish was one of the five people inside it, crammed with his back to the direction of travel between a Mexican ranch hand and a squat and odoriferous Papago squaw. Facing him more congenially if not with more comfort rode a girl in her late teens and a hawk-nosed man with a droopy mustache upon whose

31

vest gleamed the badge of a U.S. marshal.

Irish, clean-shaven now, was clothed in the black of a gambler which, if not entirely new, at least had plenty of wear left in it. The sleeves of the coat were beginning to shine at the elbows and the black string tie showed too many ironings. But Irish was satisfied. He had altered his appearance twice since meeting Lowe and figured the tinhorn look of him now to be the safest guise he could manage. Folding hands in his lap he closed his eyes, swayed and jolted.

At the Orozco Ranch, where they stopped to change horses before the long climb through the hills to the west of them, Irish opened his lids to find the coach deserted save for himself and the girl.

Her slim face, flushed and damp from heat, held the preciseness and perfection of a cameo. He was reminded rather fancifully of a pictured likeness he'd once seen of the Egyptian, Nefertiti. This girl's grey eyes—or were they actually hazel?—were not perhaps as obliquely fashioned, but the slant was there, and the pride and assurance.

Chestnut hair—sorrel, a cowman would have called it—ran flawlessly back at either side of a saucy hat to a wavy knot of down-dangling curls that, in this last of the sunlight, showed the luster of mahogany. She was slender but full-bodied and he thought her lips looked suspiciously red.

Though she was gazing very determinedly ahead of her he conceived the impression she'd been covertly studying him. He guessed she was of an age in which an older man's attention would prove flattering and exciting.

Again closing his eyes he went back in his thinking to his life as a 'high roller'—a term accorded none but the most accomplished of gamblers. No ordinary breed, representing as these did the shrewdest, crookedest bunch of scoundrels ever to prowl the western frontier.

Theirs was not a trade to be learned overnight. Irish had been an acknowledged master, which meant, of necessity, he was an expert shot and a consummate actor. The graveyards were filled with gamblers who hadn't been. These lesser lights mostly were contemptuously called 'tinhorns' and this was what Irish was got up to be taken for. At the last moment, just before boarding the stage, he had acquired and put on a pair of rimless flat-topped spectacles.

He was a man who played his hunches.

Long before he was grown Bert Irish had discovered he'd have a tough row to hoe so long as he remained within his father's sphere of influence.

Through each ascending grade of school until he'd reached the middle of his seventh he'd had to lick or be licked by every bully in the room. He'd been expected to uphold things he had not cared two hoots about, to be a model scholar and a Christian and a gentleman. When he had rebelled and veered to the other extreme 'through cussedness' he'd been hemmed with saws and aphorisms until he'd fairly felt like puking.

Irish had been a preacher's kid. He knew all about hell from first-hand experience. He had prayed every night and, after he had been tucked into bed and the lights were out, he had prayed much more earnestly under his breath. *Dear God: Give me muscles and more padding and a longer reach like Kelley. Make me ugly as Skeeter Jeems and don't, for Christ's sake, let me be a sissy.*

When he was twelve Bert ran away. It had been a planned project, brought about by an event which even now, in his mind, he shied away from. He'd gone off with a bunch of gypsies. These had not proved in the least romantic. He cut loose of them, wishing he had gone to sea. In Indiana he'd been a hay hand. In Missouri he had worked five months for a grocer. In Arkansas he'd had his first taste of ranch life and had found it hard work. He'd been thirteen then, and the following year he had gone into Texas with visions of joining the Texas Rangers. This hadn't panned out; being unable to stomach ridicule he had never been able to like them again.

He was fifteen when he reached New Orleans, man grown and knowing very well by then in which direction his real talent lay. For about eight months before leaving Texas he had fetched and carried for an aging gambler known as Blackwater Bill. Bill was a cardsharp. An expert when sober, a too steady application to the bottle had reduced him to where an employer wouldn't tolerate him beyond the second week. But he had certainly known cards and Bert had proved an apt pupil. By the time a corset drummer's bullet had put a very black period to old Bill's career, Bert had got to where he figured he could strike out on his own.

He got his first job at Houston, but was cleaned before the week was up. It was from there he'd gone to New Orleans. Gambling in the Crescent City was practically a religion. He got a job straight away, but it had nothing to do with card playing. His work was spittoons and sawdust; he emptied and sprinkled for one solid year, continuing to practice every moment of spare time, before a fortunate break in another man's health got him his place at the coveted table. He got by and that was all. When the boss got the chance to hire another professional Bert was put back to swinging a floor mop. He quit in a rage and moved on to another place.

He remained in New Orleans for about

three years, continually studying and practising, determined from the start that he would make his mark. When he wasn't playing he'd either be watching some topnotcher or perfecting new techniques and variations.

A man had to be butter-smooth and snake-quick. When you sat into a game where the sky was the limit your first mistake was likely to be your final one. It wasn't essential that you be a crook, but you had to know every dodge crooks used. Every shift of dealing, shuffling and cutting.

Step by step Bert moved up the ladder. When he wasn't behind a table he was practising his 'draw.' He begrudged every minute he was not in operation. He began to gaunt up. He was warned about consumption. When his hands began shaking he knew he'd got to let go of things.

He took a five months' vacation. Most of this he spent riding packet boats. This was the life. This was where he belonged. A continuous flow of fresh money traveled up and down that river and he watched a good deal of it painlessly changing hands. A gentleman's game and no roughnecks or racket. Their gullibility was incredible. A new crop of suckers every time the boats put out.

Then the war came along. Everything was changed. The packets began hauling freight and troops. Bert went back to the honkytonks of Front Street.

When the war was over the South was ruined, but the West, Irish suspected, was headed for a boom. He was at Abilene, Kansas, when it became the big trail town, a tin-and-tarpaper gold mine to a man of his bent.

He followed the steel rails deeper into the waving grass of the endless prairies. Each short-lived construction camp knew and felt his presence. He piled up great stakes and lost them when his luck went. At Dodge his roll figured close to a hundred thousand and he got out of the town just ahead of an angry citizens' committee.

For a while he followed the buffalo hunters, trailing them as far south as Fort Mobeetie, where, at last fed up with their stinking craziness, he pulled out and went back to the river boats.

He spent the next pair of years on the Mississippi, and the following six on the turbulent Big Muddy. But a shooting at Fort Adams drove him on to the Yellowstone and from there he went into the Dakotas. There was no lack of wealth in the Black Hills country but his luck walked out on him. He went down through Nevada into the land of the Dons and made another big clean-up in 'Frisco, but had to get out because of an indiscreet woman. He'd been thirty-two the night he'd booked passage on Critchton's boat.

★   ★   ★

The driver's voice roused Irish. 'Leavin' in two minutes! Joe—gimme a hand with that luggage.'

The coach swayed and groaned and Irish opened his eyes. He watched the marshal twist into the seat beside the girl, stretch out his long legs and relax with a sigh. A leather-faced man in range clothes climbed in and slumped down beside Irish, twisting to stare from the window. A portly drummer in a brown derby put his weight on the step and the coach rocked again as, half stumbling over the marshal's legs, he dropped onto the cushion at the girl's other side. She caught at her hat and he mumbled an apology.

The marshal said to the man beside Irish, 'At least we're bound to be there for noon grub, Haines.'

Leather Face grunted. 'Thirty minutes late right now,' he growled; and then, staring at the girl, 'Ain't you Purdon Fick's daughter?'

The girl admitted it.

The driver climbed on to his box and cracked the whip. The teams lunged into their collars and the wheels started rolling across loose shale.

'Thought you favored him. Ain't been over to the Basin for a coon's age—ain't seen you since you was in three-cornered pants,' Haines said with a rumbling laugh, 'but I never forget a face.'

The girl showed color but she managed to smile.

'Been off to school, I reckon,' Haines pursued. 'Pretty soon be gettin' married. Tearin' off with some fool cowhand to start a herd of your own—haw-haw!'

Irish, sensing the girl's discomfort, tried to haze the talk away from her by inquiring of the marshal if the country was having much trouble with Indians.

'Not here. Most of the trouble's been over around the Dragoons. They're all peaceable here—Papagos mostly. Been Christianized more than a hundred years. Farmin' folks, Reverend.'

'Them Apaches,' Haines said, 'is the ones to watch out for. They got some rough pastimes. Army keeps coddlin' 'em. 'F I had my way I'd round up the whole lot of 'em and give 'em the powder cure. Worse'n dang wolves! Only last week they caught a couple of prospectors...'

The voices droned on. Irish closed his eyes, and his ears to the sound of them. By tomorrow noon, if he took that cut-off at Sells, he should be in spitting distance of the Mexican border.

He could have gone straight south out of Tucson and been in Nogales by midnight. This had been his original intention, but after running into Lowe he'd had to change his plans. The Border Patrol would have Nogales filled with spotters. They wouldn't have to recognize him; they'd be stopping everybody who tried to leave the country. Even San Miguel would be too risky now. But there was plenty of open range between San Miguel and La Osa.

Finding a Federal marshal on the stage had naturally startled him, but he wasn't particularly worried. While under certain conditions a marshal might be persuaded to assist local officers, those conditions were hardly operative in the case of the Bristol killing, the Federal Government being in no way involved.

The drummer was getting into the talk, but Irish paid little attention until he caught the sound of his own name. 'I don't know,' the marshal was saying. 'I'd be inclined to think Indians—'

'You don't know these bucks,' growled the leather-faced Haines, riding roughshod over the marshal's opinion. 'Ol' John Esteban— he's head man of this bunch—could track a ringtail lizard across bare rock! Routine's all right; I've sent warnings to Nogales and Tubac—done it the minute I learned Irish was in town. But I'm puttin' my chips on

John Esteban. Irish will try to get across west of Osa. If he does them Injuns'll nab him sure. Beauty about them is they wouldn't know a boundary if it hit 'em in the eye!'

'For a man who don't like Indians...' the drummer began, but right about there his wind played out, punctured by the look in Haines' pulled-around stare.

The marshal, giving no heed to the drummer, appeared to be testing Haines' remarks against experience. 'You're likely right about some of that. For a Papago, Esteban's a pretty fair tracker. If he gets on to that feller's sign he'll stay with it, boundary or no boundary. But it looks to me, sheriff, you're kind of leadin' with your chin, putting guns in the hands of a bunch of Indians and deputisin'—'

'Muzzle-loaders,' Haines grinned, 'an' I ain't deputisin' nobody. I just told John to git some of his boys an' string 'em out across that waste between Miguel an' Osa. If they spot anyone tryin' to slip across they're to flag him down an' send for me. If they should discover anyone has already gone across they're to fetch him back. That's all there is to it.'

'Plumb open and above-board,' the marshal said dryly. 'Well, it's your coon, I reckon. From all I've heard about Irish he's a pretty cagey customer. Wouldn't surprise me to learn he's still around Tucson. What do

41

you think, Reverend?'

It became apparent to Irish, when heads turned in his direction, that the marshal's remark had been addressed to him, that the man some way had mistaken him for a preacher. The fact made little impression, he being too much involved with the problems stemming out of Haines' identity as sheriff and with the greater shock of learning that already Haines had blocked any chance he'd had of getting through west of Osa.

He said, 'I believe the man will strike north and head for Canada.'

Haines snorted. But the marshal seemed to be giving the idea consideration. 'Might at that,' he nodded. 'Or at least ride his back trail till he can strike out in some better fashion. Until that man Lowe ran into him in Tucson, as I understand it, they'd lost his sign going into the Superstitions. Seems—'

'They done better'n that,' Haines grumbled. 'Picked his tracks up east of Kelvin where he'd traded for a flax-maned sorrel off one of them back-country ranchers.'

The marshal squinted. 'One thing's sure, he's got plenty of choice in direction now. He can strike north towards Florence or Casa Grande. He can go into the Rincons or the Empires, or drop south towards Patagonia, south-east towards Bisbee or Douglas. Might even duck into that country around Tombstone. It's anybody's guess. I suppose,' he said, shifting his look to the sheriff, 'you've got men watching the stage lines?'

Haines' cocksureness wilted. His eyes, for a second, showed the sickness inside him. Then he said with resurgent confidence, 'The man ain't fool enough to try anything that crazy!' He struck a fist against the side of his knee. 'You mark my words: it may take a little time, but in the end John's Injuns'll git him. That open range south of Sells is gonna draw that feller just like sweets draws ants!'

Irish, yawning, closed his eyes. He shifted his shoulders and settled back, a man doing his best to let the stage's rough jolting rest him.

'But who *is* this man Irish?' the girl asked out of the hoof sound and wheel racket. There was a bewildered concern in her voice that warmed Bert. 'What has he done to cause all this—'

'Done? Hell's fire,' the sheriff roared, quite forgetting his language, 'he gun-shot a man over a card game! Governor's son-in-law! That's what he done an', by grab, he'll hang higher'n...'

'It was about ten days ago,' the marshal took over, 'on the Colorado, over near Ehrenburg. Aboard a river packet bound—'

'But if it was on a boat...'

Haines said, 'You think the Governor

cares where it was? He had big plans for Bristol and now the guy's dead, killed over a card game by a two-bit tinhorn!'

'I wouldn't call Bert Irish by that name,' piped up the drummer. 'He's a real high roller, one of the best in the business. He piled up a hundred thousand in Dodge City—'

The sheriff's bull voice cut through his words. 'Whatever he is ain't goin' to help him now. When the Governor goes after somethin', by cripes, he gits it! There's a two thousand dollars reward up right now!'

They were climbing through fawn-colored rocks and greasewood interspersed with the occasional fluted columns of giant cactus. These last, Irish noted, were beginning to put forth buds. But his thoughts were not engrossed with the aspects either of topography or nature. Indians, he knew, would be inclined to shoot first and do their jawing later. It would be sheerest folly now to ride this stage to Sells. He'd got to get off, and the sooner the better.

'Reverend,' the marshal had called him. If these spectacles in conjunction with black clothes could fool a marshal they could probably be counted on to mislead a bunch of cowmen. He might need the girl's help but he felt pretty sure he could bank on it. Totaling up his assets he decided to take the chance.

He'd get off where the girl did. They had all heard the marshal. But, because she was young enough to be impressionable, the girl would believe and her belief would influence others. She would, in fact, provide him with a ready-made identity about as far removed from his own as could be imagined. All he'd have to do, Bert thought smugly, was to stay with the part and live up to it.

CHAPTER FOUR

Even before the stage stopped Irish had marked the two men waiting in the shadows of the station's overhang. He had also noted the way the girl's gloved hands were straightening her hat and decided this was where they'd be quitting the sheriff's company. He thought of his preacher father and the book-lined shelves of his study. His father had been a graduate of Princeton with the world's greatest thinkers at the tips of his fingers. Be a gamble, of course, but he reckoned he could cut it.

Brake blocks squealed, 'Red Post!' the driver shouted, and the locked wheels shuddered the coach to a stop. 'Twenty-five minutes. You can git hot grub right acrost the street.'

The drummer, with much grunting, was

45

the first to put his feet on ground. His derby, disengaged in the process of disembarkation, struck the floorboards, bounced, and hit the ground behind him. The girl tried to keep the laughter inside her, but the sheriff, less restrained, openly guffawed. Irish asked the marshal if this was where a man got off for the Basin. 'Yep,' the lawman said, smiling tolerantly, 'you're in the Basin right now, Reverend.'

Irish jumped up, obviously flustered. 'Dear me,' he said rather sheepishly, 'I expect I must have been dozing.' Ducking his head he stepped down, taking off his spectacles. The drummer was swearing and Irish spoke to him sharply. Then he reached back a hand.

'Permit me,' he said, helping the girl to the ground. He was surprised, looking into her shadowed face, to find she was almost as tall as himself. He held her arm a bit longer than was perhaps completely necessary.

He saw one of the pair under the overhang watching him. The girl had more poise than he had looked for. Interest reached from her glance to catch at his own and something unsettling ran strongly between them. 'Thanks,' she smiled, 'thanks for everything. Are you planning to make the Basin your home?'

'I expect,' Irish said, taking off his hat, 'that will depend on the Basin, ma'am.' A

46

twisted smile tugged his lips. He had known many women, but not the kind of woman this slender hazel-eyed girl was.

She stepped back, still considering him, said 'Thanks' again; and the soft melody of her voice, enormously stirring, stayed with him long after she had hugged the approaching rancher and gone with him— and with the man whose evident interest Bert had marked—to climb into a waiting buckboard.

Irish, covering his head again, saw the sheriff and the marshal moving past him towards the restaurant. The sheriff was still talking. Realising the last of the twilight was rapidly darkening into night, Irish reckoned he'd better see about lodgings, and was fixing to go into the station when he became aware of the drummer.

The man had ludicrously dropped to hands and knees beside the coach and with considerable muttering and wheezing appeared to be trying to make up his mind to crawl under it, his butt almost bursting from the seat of his breeches. 'Betcha five dollars, Clell,' chuckled one of the loungers, 'he can't git between the wheels.'

Irish, starting to laugh, thought better of it. He put the spectacles back on his nose. About to wheel towards the now lighted station he remembered his job in this place and swung back. 'Just a minute, brother. I'll get it for you.'

Ducking around to the rear of the vehicle he leaned down and reached out and came up with the derby. He rejoined the fat man, wiping it against the black sleeve of his coat. 'Here you are,' he smiled, holding it out.

The drummer grabbed it ungraciously, eyeing Irish suspiciously. He gave it a vigorous thumping, clapped it on, scowled again and, like an outraged elephant, went flouncing off in the direction of the eating place.

The betting man said, 'If that guy ever bumps into a pin it'll be the end of him.' The man's cronies cackled. Another of them said, 'What he needs is a chin strap.' The man Clell growled, staring hard at Irish, 'Anyone send fer you?'

Irish didn't want any trouble. This Clell had the shoulders and flexing biceps of a blacksmith. Craggy brows overhung his eyes like board awnings. 'Sky pilot, ain'tcha?'

'You don't believe I'm needed here?'

'Ain't heard of no killin's recent. Ain't been no birthin's. That girl of Fick's figurin' to git herself hitched?'

'Not that I know of.'

'So what are you here for?' Clell said, stepping nearer.

Irish, staring into those little pig eyes, could feel the sweat start, could feel the creep and cringe of his crawling muscles.

48

This, in his need to stay clear of Haines' Papagos, was one of the things he hadn't considered. Reaction of local yokels to the cloth, and of himself to the threat of bodily violence.

He could feel it welling up in him now, that hollow pounding of the heart, the creeping quiver which was prelude to nausea. The iron tentacles of his will had no control over these, they were things apart, unrelated to logic, spawn of the fight which had made him leave school, forsaking friends and family, cutting every natural tie. He put down a growing impulse towards panic, forcing himself to meet the man's stare.

'Perhaps I'm here to answer the call.'

'What call? Thought you give me to understand...'

'I'm speaking about a higher call.' Even in his own ears his voice had no body. The watching loafers crowded nearer, several grinning openly. The man who had ridiculed the drummer said, 'Betcha he'll cave just like a dropped melon.'

Irish could feel his clothes sticking to him. His eyes were burning, half blinded with sweat. His mind dived to the gun strapped under his armpit, though he knew that to show it would cancel out any chance he might have of remaining here without suspicion.

His mind, denied the gun, wouldn't

49

function. All he could do was to watch with a kind of terrible fascination the methodical upswing and downswing of the man's brutal jaw as Clell worked a wad of gum back and forth across his teeth. Not even the man's hateful grin could sting Irish into making of temper a crutch against fear. The roots of this thing had gone too deep.

A man didn't often think of fright as pain, but it could be. Bert Irish knew. It was corkscrewing into him like the thrust of a twisted knife. Bad almost as the ghastliness of feeling the bones go, the splintering teeth and all the other accompanying horrors which came out of the black miasma of the past—that past which had decided him to run away with the gypsies rather than trust his luck against the chance of repetition. The older brother of a bully he had licked had laid for Irish after school and just about half killed him. It had put Bert flat on his back for three months and given him this quirk which nothing, it seemed, could get rid of.

So now he stood, pale and trembling, dumb with the effort he put forth to keep from screaming.

Clell laughed when he saw Irish shaking. 'We got no place for your kind in this country. Be on that stage when she leaves or they'll be layin' you out on a plank with a posy.'

When Irish made no answer Clell laughed

again contemptuously and, with a jerk of the head for his friends, said, 'C'mon—I gotta git the taste of this crawfish outa me.'

Though Irish didn't watch them go he heard them. How long he stood, alone with his shaking and sweating and shame, he never knew. When he came out of it enough to take notice of his surroundings he was inside the station. He had no idea how he'd gotten there or what he'd said to the man in the eyeshade who stood consideringly, flapping a fold of yellow paper against the pigeon-holes built across the back of the counter.

'Maybe you ought to take it easy for a while. Probably somethin' you've et that hasn't set right. Might be a shot of whisky would help—get a hot one with plenty of lemon laced into it and climb into bed. That's what I'd do.'

Irish, swallowing uncomfortably, said, with the flats of his hands on the counter, 'All I'm asking you for is an answer.'

The agent shook his head. 'I'm lockin' up soon as this stage pulls out.'

Things were beginning to come back into focus. Irish took a deep breath and got hold of himself. The tramp of boots pulled sound from the outside planks and through a window he saw the pair of lawmen moving stagewards. They pulled up beyond the doorway while the marshal built a smoke.

51

'What was that name?' Irish said.

'Brocton House. They'll fix you up.' The man hung there a moment with his head twisted, listening. He pushed the paper he was holding into a pigeon-hole. His under lip was trembling. 'Maybe you better get back on that coach.'

Irish looked bleakly across the rows of empty benches to a door at the farther side. The thought went through his mind that when they'd built this station they had figured to have a boom which hadn't ever materialised. He squared his shoulders and, pushing away from the counter, passed between the dusty benches. He stepped through that piece of framed night into the murmurous wind-bent shadows of the pair of giant cottonwoods that here made everything twice as dark as natural.

Irish's mouth shaped a mirthless grimace. The man meant well, but getting back on that coach wasn't the answer to anything. Not with Haines' Papagos prowling the brush.

He touched the gun in its sling under his armpit. The night wind, cool against him, brought the smell of damp earth faintly spiced with pine and the taint of dead brush fires; and he peered hungrily southward, thinking of the border and almost tempted to risk it.

Moving east through the shadows along

the station's back wall he thought if he could get a horse he might lose himself to the north of town before Clell discovered what he was up to. It would depend, of course, on how determined the man was and whether or not the fellow Irish had seen with the girl's father was concerned. Bert hadn't missed the hard look that one had given him.

He came to the end of the wall and stopped, remembering his fleeting glimpse of the town. He knew it stretched east and west with the bulk of it spread beyond the station's west end. The saloon—Beaupre's Palace—was the last building west and presumably where Clell had taken his friends for the projected refreshment.

His mind conjured the girl's face in all its fresh young beauty. Not truly beautiful perhaps, but attractive with its oddly Oriental eyes, its dewy look of innocence. Hair like mountain mahogany. He tried to visualise how it would seem undone, recalling the unsettling look that had passed between them. He put her out of his mind.

He started forward once more and again he stopped, debating the advisability of taking a saddled horse. It would not help his pose of parson. He'd better go to the livery which was down that alley behind O'Dowd's Pool Hall; he remembered now that O'Dowd's was about midway between the Palace and the Emporium, last building to the east.

He was cutting around the station's east end towards its overhung front when the crack of a lash sent fresh teams into collars. With a grinding of cramped wheels above the harness creak and hoof sound, the stage came round and went lumbering off through its wind-lifted dust in the direction of Sells.

A vast loneliness settled over Irish, as though with the stage's departure another milestone had been passed, another decision forced upon him. Beyond the bright and empty planks that flanked the station's shedlike entrance he could see the dark raise-fronted shapes of the town's closed business houses.

There was nothing over here but the station. Its lamps went out, and Irish, still irresolute, heard the heavy slam of its glassless front door, the receding tramp of the agent's feet. Both the sheriff and the marshal had gone with the stage, yet Bert felt no lift of spirit, only the awful weight of his aloneness.

He drew a ragged breath.

The town's general store—the Emporium—stood yonder, crouched toadlike in its tatters of shadow. It was perhaps fifty yards from where he now stood. To get to the livery with any chance of avoiding Clell, his best bet was to approach it by cutting north behind the Emporium.

He raked the night with watchful eyes. The station was dark as those across-the-street store fronts, but the ground between was lemon-etched with dapples of light from the saloon.

Not till he'd moved out from the station, not until he'd cleared its shadow, did his narrowing stare pick up the man in the gloom of the Emporium's gallery. There was another unmoving shape by Schenck's barber's pole and a third man standing in the entrance of O'Dowd's.

Irish drew a deep breath and was comparatively cool again. Now that he knew what he was up against he could stand there seeing small chance of avoiding this, yet able to explore any possibility of bettering it. There was one and only one. If he could reach a horse...

A hard core of fright still howled its protest, but he moved on again, leisurely angling towards the man in the gloom of the general store's arcade. The man was fortunately near the east end of the gallery and until they knew Bert meant to round it the chances were no one would move.

Twenty yards from the Emporium Irish began to sweat in grim earnest. He was past the point of no return and stuck with whatever came of this now. If Clell's men cut him off, or if reaching the stable he failed to get a horse... The street, so sharp with danger, began to whirl about him dizzily. Faster and faster until it became a blur grooved with lines of spinning red. Then, like film, it snapped and he was back in the road, alone with his frightful need to get away. He saw the man step away from Schenck's barber's pole, and he broke into a run, swerving round the dark flank of the Emporium, the man on its gallery moving to intercept him.

The man from O'Dowd's was running straight across the building fronts. The piano in Beaupre's Palace went still and pounding boots came up out of the street. Bert bent lower, striving desperately to hurl himself past the man diving off the gallery.

Clawing arms slid off his shoulders, but the fellow's tumbling body became entangled with Bert's legs, throwing him. Fright jerked him up and slammed him into the solid blackness with the sound of those others hanging over him like a sword.

He redoubled his efforts, running as he never had thought he was able, twisting left behind the Emporium's back wall through a scrap pile of broken boxes. His lungs seemed stretched till he felt sure they must burst.

He could see the poles of the corrals just ahead now and the shapes of startled horses against the slatted light from the stables. There was no time to duck through or get over the rails. He staggered gasping along them, forced by a fence that here crowded his left to plunge straight towards the building.

He was caught in the circle of light from its lantern, trapped by the shapes of waiting men. He stumbled, shoulders sagging, and half fell against the fence, the ones who'd been chasing him closing in behind. Listening to the harsh, driven sound of his own breathing, like a wild thing he stared at the men bunched in front of him. He found Clell's face. It had the look of a devil. 'Thought I told you to git on that stage.'

The others nodded, grinning, eyes avid.

No one had to tell Irish they were going to enjoy this. A macabre relish was in the strike of their eyes, in the way they stood ringing him.

Clell's snaggle of bristles climbed to mis-shapen ears, to a bulging forehead thatched with coarse sandy hair. He was heavy and swell-chested. A spattering of freckles gave his face a brindled look and there was an atavistic pleasure in the skim-milk blue of the gloating eyes so obviously revelling in Irish's predicament.

'Don't hear good, do you?' he jeered, stepping nearer.

Irish stood like a sick dog, shivering. His tongue clung parched against the roof of his mouth and in the extremity of his terror he had an almost undefeatable impulse to abandon everything and go for his gun.

But some spark of common sense deep inside him kept the hand away and the chance was lost as the shapes, shoving and jostling, closed around him. Someone shoved him from behind, then he was reeling, everything spinning, from the shock of Clell's hurled fist. He crashed into the fence and clung there, retching, legs caving under him and mind too paralysed to function. Red fog shut in around him and there was a roaring in his ears like mighty combers rushing up a beach. Now he was being jerked forward, stopped in that motion by a second terrible impact that fused in a blinding arc through which he plunged into unfathomable blackness.

He came out of it coughing, half strangled. The whole left side of his face felt gone and the hand he brought up came away from it redly and horribly sticky. His stomach rose inside him and he retched again, the sour smell of it gagging him.

Pain came, wave on shuddering wave of it. He screamed, frantically writhing, presently discovering himself sprawled in the muck of a stable runway. He worked himself dizzily on to an elbow, bewilderedly confronted by a forest of legs. His eyes climbed unclearly, stupidly peering at lantern-lit faces completely meaningless until he saw the dripping bucket. Then his eyes found Clell and it all came back.

A hairy fist reached down and took hold of his sodden shirtfront. Irish saw Clell nod and the fist hauled him upright. It made no difference that his knees buckled. Other hands caught hold of him and held him while Clell went to work. Every time he passed out they brought him round with the bucket while Clell stood coolly whistling on his knuckles until they got Bert roused enough to understand what was happening.

Through red stringers of shining mist Clell's voice said, 'Prop him up agin' the fence.'

They hooked the back of his belt over the staves and when they stepped back Irish couldn't get his head up. He tried to twist away. 'Clell—!' He couldn't tell whether he shouted it or thought he did.

'Hear better now, do you?' Clell backed off a little to give himself room.

Irish shook his head to throw the blood from his eyes. He saw Clell coming and got up a knee. Clell jumped back, swearing. The fence came apart with a crash of snapped posts, and Irish, tangled in the wreckage, was carried through it, falling heavily. Someone yelled like a knife-cut pig and he saw Clell, monstrous in the lemon light, coming after him with a jagged timber.

CHAPTER FIVE

'Careful,' a voice warned quietly. 'Put him down on the sofa.'

Irish, conscious now but still attempting a retreat from the bleakness of reality by the childish expedient of keeping his eyes shut, felt himself let go of, heard his carriers depart.

The prickling stabs and slickness of horsehair were under him and it should have been good just to find himself lying there. It was hard for him to discover any further good in anything. He had to lock his jaws. He could not relax even mentally. The burden of shame was too close, too vivid. He could not repress a shudder of revulsion.

'He's coming around,' the dry voice said. 'You better get at those bones, Doc—'

'Prop his feet up a little and get me a blanket.'

Someone moved off and the blackness settled again. Irish moved in a maze of darkness and unintelligible sound. He recovered consciousness once more to find that he was in a comfortable bed. There was a tightness about his chest and something constricting across the middle of his face. Light footsteps moved across the room. He shut his eyes again.

'You must be starved by this time.'

Irish found it rather queer to discover he was. Food should have been the last thing he wanted. He was considerably more astonished to be able to think so clearly, to realize that he could think. He ought to be half out of his head with pain from the mauling that fellow had given him. He cringed from the thought, and the girl—it was a girl—said, 'If you're asleep, all right; but if you're not you'd better get through with this.'

He didn't open his eyes all the way right at first but attempted to reconnoitre through the screen of his half-shut lids. She caught him at it and laughed, gay as the tinkle of spur rowels. He couldn't help looking then—he had to find out if she was pretty as she sounded.

She was, in spite of the suggestion of freckles that were powdered like pollen across the bridge of her nose, a nose that was extremely decorative in itself and definitely compatible with the rest of her appearance. She was young and taffy-haired. Her eyes were the green-flecked amber of a cat's and she seemed uncommonly slender behind a dress of some pale lavender material, trimmed in white at wrists and throat, and obviously designed to make the most of her endowments.

He opened his eyes all the way and lay

watching as, turning aside to leave her tray on a chest, she dragged a chair to the bed and bent over him, fluffing up his pillows, leaving a fragrance as of lilacs in the swirl of air about him. As she straightened, stepping back, Irish said a little hoarsely, 'How did you get into this?'

'Mr Beaupre sent for me.'

'Very thoughtful of Beaupre. What brought him into it?'

'Don't you remember? Mr Beaupre broke it up. He made Clell get away from you.'

'What did he use—a crowbar?'

Her eyes crinkled up and she laughed, then told him, sobering, 'Mr Beaupre's an important man around Red Post. I think he'd like to keep you here. He says if we'd had a preacher six months ago those homesteaders never would have been driven out.'

'He likes farmers?'

'He likes business. I—I'd better get your broth,' she said.

'Broth!'

She laughed at the way his face crumpled up. 'What did you expect?' She got the bowl and a spoon and came back. 'You've been out of your head for the past three days—'

'Three days!' Irish glared.

'Mr Beaupre said you'd be in bed for a week. But Haskins—he's the doc, you know—declares you can get up tomorrow if

62

you promise to be quiet and keep out of trouble.'

Irish wasn't paying much attention to her words. He was listening rather to the tones, the throaty timbre of her voice, trying to pin down an impression of having known this girl before. This was, of course, preposterous. She wasn't the kind a man would forget. He thought briefly of the other girl, and the surprising things he'd uncovered in her rose up in comparison to mock and deride him. She wasn't the kind a man would soon forget either—though her appeal was different, he told himself, different and a great deal less obvious. He understood the one watching him as he never could hope to understand Pauline Fick.

'What's the matter with me?' he said irritably.

The girl ticked them off on slim fingers. 'You've a broken nose for one thing. There's a nasty gash in that left cheek of yours and you've two cracked ribs. Not to mention the bruises and other things Doc ain't sure of.' Her eyes crinkled again. 'He figured at first you might have a concussion, but now he thinks the most of it was shock. Preachers, he told Mr Beaupre, ain't like the common run. He allows they're geared a mite higher than most.'

'I expect,' Irish said, 'I must have looked

pretty craven—'

'Indeed you didn't!' she cried, fiercely partisan. 'You—Mr Beaupre says, "Any man with guts enough to turn the other cheek—"'

She broke off, astonished when she realised it was what she was saying that had brought on his high color. Such quaint and becoming modesty was new to her experience and she regarded him with brightening interest. 'You're starved!' she said, snatching up the bowl, and, with a look that was briskly determined, approached him.

The broth appeared to improve his spirit; at least he showed an increasing awareness. Several times while she was feeding him she caught his speculative interest, and when they were finished he asked for his clothes.

She stood up, looking down at him, her lips a little parted. He was the most interesting preacher she had ever been this near to and she wondered how it would be if he should put his arms about her. Her own cheeks warmed. She said, 'No clothes before tomorrow.'

He reached for her hand but she swerved away. Sunlight fell across her hair and Irish observed that his glance was both expected and watched for. He could feel her anxiety, grinned at her then and her smile flashed back at him brightly. She set the bowl on her tray. 'I'll make Haskins give you some meat tonight.'

She felt the pull of his stare as she crossed to the door. She knew with a fierce awareness, that he was scrutinising her down to last detail. He said as she reached for the latch, 'What do they call you?'

'Cherry,' she breathed, looking back at him. 'Pap's got four sections west of here. You rest quiet now, Parson. I'll most likely be back after Doc gets done with you.'

*　　*　　*

Haskins, when he came, clucked around like a nervous hen. He was stout, baldheaded and crowding fifty. He took the court plaster and gauze off Irish's face, peered near-sightedly and, muttering, went stomping irritably back to his bag. 'Had to take five stitches in the cheek,' he said testily. 'Prob'ly pucker some. Nose ain't goin' to look too good either, but you're lucky—damn lucky! If they'd stopped that carnival half a minute later I'd of had you stowed inside a hundred-dollar casket.'

'Could be a treat in store for you.'

Haskins sniffed and looked at him and snorted. 'Likely more to that than you figure. Last sky pilot we—'

'Tell me about Beaupre.'

'What about him?'

'Girl kind of hinted he might be one of
65

your bigger moguls.'

'Big enough,' the doctor said. 'Runs the Palace Saloon and Dance Hall—you're in the back of it now. Owns the Ophir Restaurant, the O.K. Feed & Livery and the buildin' where Schenck's got his barber shop. Got a plaster on O'Dowd's. Furniture business and the bakeshop are mine.'

'Two-man town, eh?'

Haskins, frowning, smeared salve on a stick and applied it to Irish's torn cheek. 'Have to dress that again in a couple of days.'

'Girl seemed to think Beaupre'd like to have me stay here. In the Basin, I mean.'

'He likes just about anything that'll make more noise in his cash drawer.'

'Wouldn't think he'd want me, then. Rotgut and women—'

Haskins said with a sour grin, 'He'll make you a proposition to take care of that. Wants to see this town grow. Only way it can is to get in settlers. Ranchers don't want 'em. Run the last batch out with some pretty rough treatment—leastways,' he grumbled, 'somebody did.'

He finished work on Irish's face and swept the stuff of his trade back into his bag. 'Take it easy. Don't try to get rambunctious. You can get up tomorrow and put on your clothes, but don't leave this room till after I've seen you.'

He wiped his hands and picked up the

bag. As he was leaving the bed Irish called after him casually, 'What's this man Clell do for a living?'

Haskins stared and shook his head.

'You called the tune yourself,' Irish smiled. 'Lost sheep are a parson's business. If I could help—'

'You better drop around and pick out that casket.'

*　　*　　*

Irish was a little disappointed when the girl did not return. There were too many things on his mind best kept away from for him to relish putting in the long afternoon alone. Life, he reflected, was mainly a matter of getting used to yourself and your own inabilities. Nothing was ever quite the way a person wanted it. People compromised, giving a little, taking a little, until the altered balance became something they could live with. In such fashion, over the years, he had come to be able to tolerate the burden of shame and self-loathing that inevitably marched in the wake of his fright.

He did not often give way to it to the extent he had with Clell. The tendency, of course, was always lurking, twisting his guts behind the rigid control he had to have as a gambler. In the past he had concealed it behind the crutch of his hair-triggered gun, but here, as a parson, that comfort was denied him. Still that business with Clell might yet prove a blessing. It was bound to have somewhat altered his appearance and might have strengthened the security of this role he had adopted if the rest of the Basin shared Beaupre's view.

Irish had plenty of time to wonder if he'd been wise to attempt this deception he was practising. He had the memories of his father and the things the old man had ground into him, but even with these he was on shaky footing. There was so much he didn't know—and there was this Beaupre, too, and maybe that fellow he'd seen with Purdon Fick in addition to the continuing threat of further trouble with Clell.

After a couple of hours he got up and tramped around. He was stiffer than he'd expected and being on his feet appeared to aggravate his face, but let him get rid of this giddiness and he reckoned he could make out to put up with the rest.

The girl crossed his mind again, kindling the urge he had felt in the pull of her. At the moment, however, he was more concerned with his host. Why had Beaupre stepped in to help him? What kind of game was he playing? He must know that a preacher was bound to fight the very business he coveted. And why, if he'd girls right here in this building, had he sent across the Basin for the daughter of a rancher? Because he considered Irish a parson?

Bert's father might have assumed so. Bert, not blinded by Christian concepts, was more inclined to believe the girl herself was the answer. If it was Beaupre's purpose to keep him in the country he could hardly have baited him to better advantage. But how had he persuaded the girl's folks to let her come?

He got the steak Cherry had promised at a little after six. It looked a might puny helping; the bread was stale and the potatoes greasy. The coffee proved strong enough to speak for itself. He asked the man who'd come in with the food where the girl was. The fellow looked like a swamper. The girl, he said, had been sent home with a couple of quarts for her father.

'Drinking man, is he?'

'Gor! 'E drinks like fish!' The man fingered his galluses. 'Jest leave that stuff settin' when yer done with it.'

By the time he was done with it the bit of meat seemed to Irish to have been as big as a steer. He left half the potatoes still anchored in their grease. He finished the coffee with his thoughts blackly tramping around the man who had gone to so much bother on his behalf.

It all tied in. The beating in the stableyard owned by this man Beaupre. The man's timely arrival which had stopped it short of

69

murder. The attractive nurse with the provocative equipment. The departure of the bait with the bottles for poor old pappy. Beaupre *wanted* him to follow her out there.

Irish could almost hear the wheels going round. And the beautiful thing about this rigged deal was the remarkable adroitness with which it had been handled. Whether Irish was a parson in fact or by convenience the bait, in its challenge, must seem equally attractive, even when paraded with such openly brazen effrontery.

*   *   *

Beaupre, introducing himself, came in the next day, a wiry man of medium height, dressed in black broadcloth with a tie at his throat. He had a middle-aged face, clean shaven except for the grizzled mustache beneath the broad and red-veined nose; a very ordinary face which did not warrant a second look unless, like Irish, a man was schooled to place his bets on the intangibles glimpsed in the stare of cold eyes. 'You're looking better,' he told Irish. 'How do you feel?'

'Little rocky,' Irish admitted.

'If it's any consolation,' Beaupre smiled with his mouth, 'you're lucky. That Clell,' he said, sighing, 'is a bad actor, Parson.'

Favoring his left foot he pulled the tails of

70

his coat up and, moving back the chair a way, sat down, adjusting his trouser legs. He said, thoughtfully frowning at the shine of his boots, 'I'd not be very much surprised if he'd had more than a little to do with getting rid of those farmers I got in here about a year ago.'

'What's Clell do for a living?'

'Odd Jobs.'

'Like the kind he did on me?'

'More or less.'

'Are you suggesting someone paid for that?'

Beaupre's eyes stabbed out from under their brows. 'He's capable of doing that on his own. You got any reason for thinking someone might have?'

Irish said, 'That was a remarkable young lady you had here looking after me. She do that sort of thing regularly?'

'Cherry?' Beaupre chuckled. 'She doesn't do anything regularly. Father's a ranchman. Fardel. Owns Crescent.'

'I'm surprised you were able to induce such a girl to come to a place of this kind.' Irish's tone let it be known that he considered it rather shocking.

Beaupre said, steepling his fingers, 'Girl's restless. Nothing around Crescent she could set much store by. Old man's a stubborn cuss—hell on the whisky. Native of Philadelphia. People had money, gave him a good education; had a girl all picked out for him. Run off with a hill woman. Seems like hills and engineering didn't ever get blended proper.'

'What about the girl's mother?'

'Reckon I'll let you judge for yourself. You'll be seeing them all,' Beaupre said. 'They're part of your flock.' He considered Bert Irish with an amused speculation, watching him from under the tufted crags of grey-streaked brows. 'Name's Chloe. You'll be preaching here, won't you?'

'What happened to the last parson?'

'Opinions differ,' said Beaupre gravely. 'Jack Horner, one of the Straddlebug riders, claims to have seen him west of Pine Holler. This was just about the time I was bringing in those settlers. Preacher—according to Horner—was pointed north in sorghum and feathers on a bullet-creased roan that was travelling due south. By the way, I found your spectacles. Guess you'll be having to invest in a new pair. Can't help you on that, but I've got some new clothes for you.'

'You know,' Irish said, looking into the man's cold stare, 'I never would have taken you for a do-gooder, Beaupre.'

The saloon-man laughed and got up. Reaching inside his coat he produced Irish's pistol rolled up in its shoulder sling and gently laid it on the chair.

'I'm a business man, Parson. I think we'll

72

get along.'

CHAPTER SIX

Irish was no nearer knowing what he'd better
do at breakfast than he'd been the night
before watching that door shut back of
Beaupre.

While waiting for Haskins he got the pistol
from its harness under the pillow and
carefully went over it. The gun was fully
loaded except for the chamber under the
hammer, and so far as he could determine
the loads had not been tampered with.

He put the gun away and got up in his
borrowed nightshirt and stood at the room's
single window staring out at the bright shine
of bottles glinting up through the weeds of
the unkempt backyard. The drought-stricken
range stretched leprously mottled in earthy
ochres to the sunlit peaks of purple
mountains north and east. West loomed the
towering crags of the Comobabis—called so
at least on the map he'd studied when in
Tucson he'd been hunting a way to get south
of the border without running into the arms
of the law.

North of these and apparently merging
with the Roskruge chain from the right were
the Vacca Hills, grayly blue from this point,

73

with the serrated rim of the Santa Rosas faintly discernible above and beyond them.

Irish, glumly wondering about his money-belt, got back into bed.

Haskins didn't come that day and by the time he had breakfasted the following morning he was in a real sod-pawing mood. He meant as quickly as possible to get hold of a horse and while ostensibly making the acquaintance of his parish do what he could to fix this country better in mind. Though he was not planning any imminent departure he deemed it well to know where he'd be running if he had to.

He should have bought that map. Playing the part of a parson had not seemed too difficult when the marshal's mistake had given him the notion; but there were, he was now forced to realise, far too many things he didn't know about these people, the wheels-within-wheels politics which had been suggestively lurking behind that talk he'd had with Beaupre.

Remembering the man's hard and calculating stare it was obvious Anton Beaupre had not saved Bert's life out of charity. Whatever the man was up to he was counting on help from Irish. Each small thing he had done, each declaration, cried its warning of danger through the worrying confusion which had got into Irish's thinking. And he was not forgetting the look with which the man had returned his pistol.

How much did Beaupre guess? He would have realised, at least, the extreme incongruity of a parson with a gun cached under his armpit.

When Haskins showed up, about the middle of the morning, he seemed in as short a humour as Irish was himself. He examined Bert in scowling silence, brusquely replacing the bandages with fresh ones. He ordered Bert up, made him move around while he considered him critically. 'Wednesday I'll take those stitches out. You can put on your duds and stay up if you want to.'

'When can I move out of here?'

'I wouldn't be in any hurry about it.'

The tone of that remark pulled Irish up, narrowly staring.

Haskins said, 'You picked a hell of a time to come into this country. If you can take good advice you'll stay out of circulation till some of this dust around here gets settled.'

'Dust?'

'I guess *blood* would be a better word. Straddlebug's feelin' the pinch of this drought. They've put two men to homesteading range that has always been used by Crescent. There's apt to be trouble. And bad trouble, likely, if Fardel can get anybody to side him.'

'A range war?'

'Prob'ly won't come to that.' Haskins

75

scowled. 'Straddlebug's too big for any man with sense to monkey with. But Fardel's stubborn.'

Testily, seeing Irish's lack of comprehension, he explained the situation. Fick, who bossed Straddlebug (a syndicate property headquartered in Chicago) had too many cattle for grass currently available within his control. Crescent, Fardel's spread, had more grass than it could use in the next three years, and water; whereas Fick was worse up against it for water than he was for feed even. It was an explosive collection of circumstances, aggravated, according to Haskins, by Fardel's own bullheadedness. 'The man's no rancher. He's been enjoying Fick's headache. He could have leased Fick that range and avoided this whole business.'

'What's the matter with him?' Irish said, sitting down again.

'Told you. Chuckle-headed as a prairie dog! Calls Fick "that damn buggy boss." They never did hit it off from the time Fick come in here. Them girls,' he said, shaking his head, 'might be part of it.'

'Fardel's range open to homesteading?'

'Whole country's open. All Fardel owns is the six hundred and forty covering the source of his water. If those fellows lease to Straddlebug—which is certainly what they're figurin' to do—Fick's cows will use Crescent water. First critter Fardel takes a gun to will be all the excuse McCartrey needs—'

'McCartrey?'

'Straddlebug range boss.'

Irish described the fellow who had been with Fick at the station.

'That's him,' Haskins nodded. 'A damn exterminatin' sonofabitch that's gettin' a heap too big for his britches!' He snapped his bag shut and picked up his hat. 'If you want some real *good* advice you'll do what Clell told you to do.'

'Clell?' Irish stared. 'But Beaupre—'

'Sure. Big man around Red Post; got a lot of big ideas. But outside of town he don't pack enough weight to stagger a June bug. You didn't see Clell pickin' on that drummer, did you?'

*   *   *

Fick's daughter, Pauline, stood by the day corral at Straddlebug idly talking with her father while one of the hands threw a saddle on a blaze-faced roan the girl had indicated would suit her. Fick had thought the horse might be more than she could handle after being so long away from the ranch, but she had laughed at his fears and the hand had declared admiringly, 'Miz Polly kin ride anythin' with hair.'

She was lovely today in a calico blouse and a split riding skirt of buff-colored suede. She had her hair put up in the latest Virginia fashion and the cluster of curls above the blue silk scarf she had tied about her neck held the sun-struck gleam of mahogany. She had her hat in her hand and her father said dryly, 'You better put that on if—' and broke off, staring intently towards where dust was building above the trail climbing out of the Basin.

The girl turned her head to look more closely at her father, noticing how he had aged this past year; discovering almost with a sense of shock how gray he was getting about the temples—even his beard was beginning to turn. And there was a network of wrinkles about his eyes that had not been apparent when she'd left last fall.

She put on her hat and adjusted the chin strap, aware of the ranch hand's open admiration. He brought her horse from the corral, leaving the animal on grounded reins, and stared like her father at the approaching dust. 'Chunks, I reckon,' he said to Fick. 'Bates sent him to town for a new rope last night.'

McCartrey came up and Fick said without turning, 'He always run the hoofs off his horse?'

'He's all right,' McCartrey said. He let the corners of his glance travel over the girl, grinning when he saw her tightened chin start to climb. 'Goin' to look the place over?'

'I'd thought about it.'

The words came out more stiffly than she'd intended and she couldn't fight back the flush that came into her cheeks with his chuckle. She looked at him now, very direct and head on. The glint in McCartrey's eyes changed subtly, but she had seen the amusement and stared angrily at him until he shifted his glance towards the oncoming rider, now plainly visible and belatedly slowing to a more seemly pace.

McCartrey had finally shaved, a concession from a man who never took off his hat in the presence of a woman. Though of middle height, he was, in the parlance of local tradition, big enough to hunt bears with a switch. And arrogant enough to, also, she decided. There wasn't a man on the payroll he couldn't lift with one fist; and all of them jumped when he spoke, even these new ones like this fellow Chunks.

She looked at the range boss with her hands unconsciously fisting. Black hair, black eyes and a weather-burnt skin that, she sometimes thought, was like the hide of a rhinoceros. Yet the man had charm. When he chose to use it.

Chunks came up, his glance moving to McCartrey. Pauline saw the hot color surging up through her father's whiskers, the bulge of his eyes and forward hunching of the shoulders beneath brown herringbone as he reached for the man's bridle. 'By God, sir,' he roared, 'when a man rides for me he takes *care* of his horses! What do you think you're doing, riding a horse in this heat like that?'

The man's eyes swivelled down and then back to McCartrey. 'Big excitement in town, Bates. Clell just about half killed that new parson—couple nights ago it was. They're all talkin' about it. Feller, they tell me, looked like he'd been through a meat grinder. Clell woulda kilt him if Beaupre hadn't broken it up. Beaupre's takin' care of him—of the parson, I mean. Got the Fardel girl to come in and—'

'Town marshal arrest Clell?'

Chunks grinned. 'Give him hail Columbia. Told him to git plumb out of town an' not come back till he could act like a gentleman. Reckon that amounts to banishment, don't it?'

'You see the storekeeper about those supplies?'

'What supplies?' Fick growled, swinging round to face McCartrey.

'That stuff for Jack an' Joe. I sent 'em over there this mornin'—might's well get the wheels to turnin'. What you wanted, wasn't it?'

Pauline looked at him sharply, not liking the inflection he put into that question. Through a tightening stillness she heard the

80

bawling of cattle. Fick stood hunched like a prodded bull. The familiar brown coat appeared oddly too large for him and there were undercurrents here she could feel but not get hold of. It almost seemed in that moment as though her father were afraid of McCartrey. This was ridiculous, of course, but...

Fick said harshly, 'You sent that damned Kid...'

'I sent a pair that could get the job done.'

'Knowing that Kid...'

'You worry too much,' McCartrey said smoothly. His voice roughened. 'We'll get nowhere flubbin' around with this. When you've got a thing to do, then do it an' get it over with. That's my notion—but you're the boss. You got better ideas right now's the time to air 'em.'

Behind the heavy Civil War mustache McCartrey's mouth looked curved in derision. It wasn't, of course. This was some trick of the light. Even so, Pauline was startled by the change in her father. The skin of his cheeks was like gray clay. He seemed almost to stagger as he turned to move off.

McCartrey called, 'Have you?'

Fick shook his head and kept going. Pauline wondered if he were sick. She started to go after him, and McCartrey, dismissing Chunks, stepped in front of her. 'If you're goin' for a ride,' he said, 'I'll go with you.'

'Perhaps I'd prefer to ride alone.'

He considered her, smiling. 'You used to want to have me ride with you.' When she continued to look hostile he said wistfully, half frowning, 'What's happened to us, Polly? Has bein' away made this much difference? I can remember last summer...'

Her agitation was not lost on him. She saw the hard white flash of his teeth and tried to stare him down. But in the end, with burning cheeks, it was her glance that swerved aside. 'It's not going to happen again.'

He stepped closer, big, confident, sure of himself. 'Now is that any way to—'

'Bates,' she said angrily, 'let go of me.'

He stepped back, a tolerant amusement in the glance that watched her. 'Listen, girl—'

'I listened last summer. I've had all winter to understand what a fool I was.'

'You're all mixed up,' McCartrey said, bold eyes still running over her. 'There was reasons why—'

'I'm sure of that.'

The scorn in her eyes was wasted on him. His experience discounted her contempt in advance. 'Say the word,' he grinned, 'and we'll be hitched next week.'

Pushing past him she went towards the house without answering.

CHAPTER SEVEN

Irish sat a good while on the side of the bed with bare feet on the floor after the doctor's departure. If what Haskins had told him concerning Crescent and Straddlebug came within hog-calling distance of the truth it posed a challenge which, as the Basin's new parson, he'd be expected to look into.

He cursed the marshal's careless assumption which had caused him to embark on this preposterous deception, and wondered with growing disquiet how long he'd have before the fireworks. Wasting no thought on the advice the doctor had given him, he centered, frowning attention on the implications of the man's parting shot.

Obviously Haskins believed Clell had been hired to kill him. Considering Beaupre's subsequent actions it seemed foolish to imagine he'd had anything to do with it. This brought Irish's thinking back again to McCartrey, the man whose hard stare he had noticed while talking with the Straddlebug manager's daughter. Yet why should Fick's range boss have it in for a total stranger?

Grimly thinking about it Irish decided there might be a number of reasons. This land grab, for one thing. The girl herself. Or the simple fact that Bert was a stranger and that someone around here several months ago had run Beaupre's settlers out of this Basin.

The cattle crowd, according to Haskins' suspicions. And who, Irish thought, recalling McCartrey's stare, would be more likely to boss operations than this man whom the doctor, in a moment of unguarded anger, had called bluntly an 'exterminating sonofabitch'?

If, as Haskins had said, the country was open to settlement, McCartrey might very well be anticipating government intervention and have taken this means of protecting himself.

But it was Beaupre right now that had Bert fighting his hat. The fellow's place in this picture was about as disconcerting as Bert's memory of that squatter selling him back his own gun.

At around half past eleven the swamper came in with a platter of steak busily sizzling in onions and garnished with potatoes. There was a whole pot of coffee, too, and by the time Bert had put these away the man was back with a well-pressed suit of black broadcloth, the cleaned hat Bert had worn and a fresh set of underthings.

Irish lost no time getting into these. They were an extremely good fit, proving the accuracy of Beaupre's observation. The shirt, of white linen, was utterly without frills. The tie was a black Ascot and the cut of the suit more in keeping with clerical standards than the outfit Clell had ruined. Bert's money-belt was with these things, still reasonably heavy, and in one of the pockets of the coat he found a limp-backed dog-eared Bible, complete with black ribbon for keeping one's place.

At fifteen minutes after noon Irish walked into the Brocton House, the town's only hotel. The clerk pushed the book at him. *Reverend Barton* was what he wrote, and the clerk, adjusting his sleeve guards, said, 'Proud to have you with us, Preacher. We're puttin' you in the "Bridal Suite"—'

'One small room is all I'll need. On the ground floor—'

'Sorry. Mr Beaupre left very definite orders. You've the whole front end of the second floor.' He pushed a key in Bert's direction. 'Room Thirteen will let you in.'

Irish managed to hide his annoyance. Picking up the key he was moving stairwards when a man came in through the glare off the street. 'Where's Doc?' he demanded with a great stir of dust. 'Ain't in his store an' ain't in the restaurant. Miz Fentriss over to Pine Holler's hevin' pains...'

The clerk, fanning at the dust, said testily, 'Try the bakeshop. If he's around at all you'll likely catch him there.'

The man went hurrying into the street.

Irish, more used up than he'd imagined, paused and stood darkly frowning when his hand touched the banister. He came back as far as the cigar case. 'Where's that?'

'Pine Holler?' The clerk looked down his nose. 'You ain't in no shape to go traipsin' out there. No point to it anyway. Them people's used to pains—hev 'em reg'lar as clockwork. You won't catch Doc wearin' out no hoss on that road.'

Irish, hand on the gritty case, regretfully denied himself the solace of a smoke. He took the hand away and felt the Bible in his pocket. "'They that wait upon the Lord shall renew their strength; they shall mount up with wings as eagles,'" he quoted sardonically, and followed the departed man into street.

*   *   *

It was late afternoon of the following day when Bert, after a bite at the restaurant, staggered up to his rooms and slept the clock round. He got up feeling stiff but more like his old self. After scrubbing the road grime off his body he got into his clothes and was crossing the lobby when the clerk crooked a finger. 'Mr Beaupre was by a couple times and there's this letter. How'd you find things at the Holler? Fentrisses got enough now for a ball team?' He appeared to think this was extravagantly funny until he discovered Irish's cold-faced silence. He looked a little startled then. 'Somethin' stuck in your craw?'

'Mrs Fentriss,' Irish said, 'didn't make it.'

The street looked forlornly forsaken at this hour. Heat curled off the scarred plank walks and where there weren't any walks it shimmered and danced in the intense white glare. He went into the Ophir, pre-empting a table that commanded a view of the door and windows, telling the girl he'd have whatever was ready. She looked at him curiously. 'Ain't you the new parson?' Irish said rather grimly that he reckoned he was.

He tried to give his attention to the food and shelve his problems, but the thought of Cherry Fardel kept nagging him like an aching tooth. He was convinced he had known or at least seen her before and it vexed him to be unable to pin down the elusive details. Perhaps, he reflected, the doctor had been more right than he knew in ascribing to the girls at least a part of Fardel's antagonism towards Fick and the ranch he operated. A man could do some damned foolish things when pushed hard enough by resentment.

He ought to see Fick, he supposed without enthusiasm. If Haskins' assumptions were correct there was bound to be trouble. Certainly if Straddlebug had put those men on Crescent, Fick could pull them off. As resident manager Fick had the authority, and, if his need was grass and water, he might at least give Irish a chance to negotiate.

The biscuit-shooter came back with his food. 'Seen the medicine man yet?' she asked, putting the sugar and canned cow within reach. 'Come in yesterday,' she smiled as Irish looked up in obvious ignorance. 'Lordy! That feller's better than a circus. Claims that stuff in them bottles—'

She broke off, unconsciously frowning, as a man rode past on an apron-faced bay whose work-roughened coat was dull with dried lather. A pair of brush-scarred chaps flapped forward of the saddle. The man's legs were encased in grimy corduroy trousers stuffed into fancy-topped boots behind whose run-over heels the big rowels of silver spurs set up an intermittent flashing. The man was weedy built with a sharp and bony face, and, though he must have been in his teens, there was such viciousness in the pale look of his stare the girl beside Irish shivered.

'Who is he?' Bert said.

The girl looked down at him, shuddering. 'That horrible Kid ...' She rubbed cold arms and moved off, heading back of the counter. 'It's time that fool marshal did something about him...'

Beaupre came in and, discovering Irish,

came over and pulled out a chair. Settling into it he said, 'You don't have to break your neck getting started.'

Irish went on with his eating. While he was buttering a second piece of bread he looked thoughtfully at the saloon man. 'You think perhaps a new broom might tend to swing a bit too lively?'

'You wouldn't enjoy a relapse.'

Irish forked some more food into his mouth and chewed steadily. After he had swallowed he sluiced his throat with some coffee. 'You're thinking sooner or later I'll get around to the Palace.'

Beaupre grinned blandly. He bit the end from a cigar and fired up.

Irish said, 'Where's the meeting house?'

'What I mean. No sense rushing yourself into a corner.'

Irish said thinly, 'Let me get this straight. Are you under the impression I can't deliver a sermon?'

Beaupre resettled the crease of his trousers. 'You won't want to preach till you've got rid of those bandages—'

'I'll be rid of them tomorrow.'

'—and you'll be needing some new spectacles.'

'I can get along without them.'

'Rather imagined you could when I found they were nothing but window glass.'

The silence turned thick while they

considered each other. 'Window-glass spectacles and a gun in a shoulder rig. Useful—like that money-belt,' Beaupre said softly. 'But hardly what a man would look to find on a parson.'

'Chew it finer,' Irish said.

'Your friend Clell drifted back into town this morning.'

'He'd been away?'

Beaupre, grinning, steepled his finger. 'We could do some real traveling. In double harness.'

'Where were you thinking of going, Mr Beaupre?'

'Might go to the sheriff if you keep fighting the bit. Ever think about that?'

'A gone goose,' Irish smiled, 'makes a mighty poor supper.' He dropped some coins on the table and got out of his chair.

'That all you got to say to me?'

'I might add a few words but they wouldn't change anything.'

Beaupre's eyes watched him lazily. 'Go ahead,' he invited.

Irish put on his hat. 'You're barking up the wrong tree.'

*   *   *

The sun, when he stepped into the street, still lacked a few minutes of reaching the west rim. Irish found his jaws clenched. It

90

wasn't hot, but he was sweating. He raked a bitter look up and down the sand-scoured store fronts and wished he had never heard of this place. He scrubbed a hand across his cheek and abruptly angled towards the livery. He saw a buckboard coming behind a pair of trotting bays, and fishing out the letter the clerk had given him tore it open. *Come out to the ranch. I've got to see you.* No name was signed but he remembered the fragrance—the lilacs he'd smelled when Cherry Fardel had fluffed up his pillows.

He scowled and stopped, and then went on again, feeling the lure of her even now. The smouldering interest looking out of her stare, the pantherish grace of all her movements and that shining eager recklessness so restively tethered behind the quick hungers. In this too thin girl the juices of life made a tumultuous uncontainable cataract, too demanding, too determined to leave her trapped many more days in the dreary uneventfulness of her present isolation. She was ripe to break over, to welcome any hand that might tend to set her free.

Irish, frowning, thrust the note in his pocket. He thought again of going to Fick; he even considered going to Crescent as he prowled the scuffed planks of the walk. Not to abet the girl's romantic illusions but to talk, if he could, a little sense into her head, to explain that the world wore the same face everywhere. He thought, too, it might advantage him to look in on these Straddlebug homesteaders.

The buckboard was nearer now, coming directly towards him, having left its former course which would have terminated at the Emporium. A girl was driving the half-wild team; a pair, by the looks, which had been caught up from some ranch's saddle band. He stared again at the girl and knew her, even in calico blouse and buff skirt and that blur of blue which showed at her throat—knew by the hair that in this last blaze of sunlight held the bright gleam of copper.

He started to turn and she called and he stopped, unaccountably not wanting to. He took off his hat when she pulled up alongside, watching her wrap reins about the whip socket and, twisting around, look down at him with the eyes he remembered gravely searching his face.

He tried to find something to say and could not, and the eyes that reminded him so strongly of Nefertiti did not smile but continued to appraise him in a way that became even more disconcerting. He growled stiffly, 'You wanted to see me?'

'We heard,' she said, nodding, 'about your ... trouble I—I didn't want you to think Dad had anything to do with that.'

She must have read the astonishment in his glance. Confusion made her own veer away while a deeper color crept over her cheeks and he saw the twist of her hands in her lap.

He stood considering these things and said in a tone that was suddenly bleak, 'Why would Purdon Fick imagine I might hold him responsible?'

'Oh, he didn't—believe me. I'm sure it never occurred to him...'

'But it occurred to you. I'm wondering why.'

He didn't make a question of it but the question was there, hovering between them, uncomfortably demanding an answer. The flush faded out of her cheeks, and her eyes, staring down at him, looked darkly enormous. He was reminded of a time another boy and himself had been caught stealing pears; the same expression was in her face that he had observed on his companion's, the same bewildered uncertainty, the same suggestion of panic.

The team felt it, shifting nervously. A bit of tattered paper—the envelope he'd discarded?—suddenly fluttered from an alley, was caught in a lifting cross-draft and whipped between their legs.

Both horses spooked, went off the ground and came down lunging into their collars. The reins tore loose and before she could catch them were gone, flying wildly, as the team broke into a savage run.

Irish jerked free the reins of a horse at the tie rack, hand going to the horn. But the animal, excited, shied away as he tried for the stirrup. By the time he was mounted the clattering buckboard was bouncing and bounding towards undoubted destruction. He heard doors banging open, a babble of voice sound. Someone yelled, *'Runaway!'* and a man dived into the street from the pool hall trying to intercept them, but the horses, veering, kept going, running harder, the buckboard creening crazily behind them. Past the Palace they swept, the racket of their hoofs dropping off the walls like thunder; Irish, reins slashing, after them.

He could see the girl precariously clinging to the seat, hat gone, hair plumed out like the tails of the frantic horses. They had left the road. A scant hundred yards ahead the dark lip of an arroyo cut diagonally across their path. If the team went into that ditch...

He quit using the reins, settling down to grim riding, employing every dodge he had learned as a cowboy to crowd more speed from the borrowed horse. The horse, responding, was overhauling them now, but the black gash of the erosion was looming perilously close and there was yet twelve feet between Bert's reach and the heads of the bolting team. With spurs on his heels he might have had a chance, but he knew the way it was he wasn't ever going to make it.

He spoke to the horse, encouraging it, and gained another yard. The arroyo now was but a reata's length away and he was afraid to grab the rein ribboning past lest it throw them into the very crash he was striving so desperately to avoid.

There was no possibility of reaching their heads now. Tearing alongside the blur of the near wheel he did the only thing he could. Kicking feet from the stirrups he stood up and jumped.

His left shin struck the side of the box, spilling him insecurely across the frame, where he clung, half paralysed, until he could get enough purchase to haul himself aboard. His leg felt like a club had struck it, but he clambered up and over the seat past the white-faced girl and, with jaws locked together, stepped on to the doubletree, wedging himself between the two runaways, swaying and jouncing as he worked down the tongue till he could get a hand on the checklines where they crossed behind the crazed horses' withers.

He stabbed a quick look ahead.

The broken rim of the drop was less than thirty feet away when he spoke to the horses, taking a firm grip but easing them gently, exerting only enough pressure to get them in hand. They were still too jittery. But he couldn't wait any longer.

Steadily putting more pressure on the near rein he swung them into the start of a circle, hearing the shuddering screech of racked timbers as the full hurtling drive of weight and momentum came against the turn of grinding wheels. For a sickening instant he felt the whole right side of the buckboard come up, teetering on the verge of capsizing. He saw the gut of the crevice swaying dizzily below them, then the wheels settled back and took hold and they were out of it, away from the brink in the slackening completion of the turn he had started.

He stopped the team, blowing and covered with lather, in front of the Palace, and, vaulting over the off horse, limped around to their heads, speaking soothingly to them till they were calm enough to stand.

'I'd take a rasp to them damn fools!' somebody snarled.

People crowded round the buckboard. Anton Beaupre, resplendent in a bottle-green coat, was helping the shaking girl to the ground, Haskins hovering querulously at his shoulder, by the time Irish elbowed a way through the curious. Pauline's face was like paper, but she managed a wan smile as she disengaged herself from the saloon-keeper.

A man came pushing forward as the fluttering doc was about to pilot the girl away from the jabbering crowd. This was a gangling bony individual with the down of adolescence blurring the angles of a face prematurely etched with the hallmarks of hard living. Irish recognized him at once as the fellow the Ophir waitress had called 'that horrible Kid.' His eyes were old and dark with evil and the crowd fell away from him—all but Beaupre.

He demanded, frowning, 'What do you want, Horner?'

'I'm takin' her home. What the hell do you think?'

'She's in no condition—'

'She ain't been no more than shook up a mite. You think,' Horner said with an open hostility, 'her ol' man wants—'

'I'm staying in town,' Pauline said with her chin up. 'With the Bessingers,' she added, eyes defiant behind their glow of resentment as the gangling Kid continued to glower. She swung away from him then, her glance seeking Irish. It looked somehow different, some way brighter when it found him. 'I haven't thanked you...' she began, but he headed her off, saying gruffly, 'A man does what he has to,' and inclined his head stiffly, too aware of the Kid's sharpened scrutiny.

The sun was down now, the evening shadows thickening, but light streaming out from the Palace's lamps seemed to heighten the auburn gleam of her hair, which she had somehow managed to put into a semblance of order. It brought out the ivory tints of her skin, playing tricks with his thinking and disturbing him further. He saw with surprise that she was smiling.

'Of course,' she said quietly, quite as though they were alone. 'You will not, however, be able to sidetrack Dad; he'll insist on meeting his obligations. In the meantime I'd like to have you meet the Bessingers...' Her smile trembled a little. 'We'll expect you about eight.'

She moved off with old Haskins clucking testily beside her.

The crowd began to break up. A man slapped Irish's shoulder. 'You done all right, Parson.'

He caught Beaupre's enigmatic stare. The man stepped nearer. 'Make the most of it.'

Irish was turning away when a hand grabbed his arm, roughly whirling him.

He looked into the scowling face of the Kid.

CHAPTER EIGHT

Bates McCartrey was a pretty shrewd customer who could size up a man about as well as he could a heifer and was generally regarded as the Basin's most eligible bachelor. With women, as with politics, he was in the habit of playing the field, being too cagey to be pinned down and too ambitious to be swayed by scruples. He stayed on with Fick because his job as Straddlebug range boss gave him not only prestige but advantages he could have had with no other outfit.

He banked his paychecks and built up this backlog with the proceeds of short-counting Straddlebug trail herds and an unsuspected dexterity in the application of a heated cinch ring. He collected mavericks and ran his own brand with Fick's knowledge. Fick conceded this privilege as a means of securing his allegiance—a real laugh. In six years Bates McCartrey had grown fat on this job and could and would long since have got rid of the manager but for the view that Fick made such an excellent scapegoat. When the chips were down Bates aimed to own the spread; it had been just around the corner when Pauline had come back with the damned interloper.

McCartrey admitted a mistake with that fellow; the mistake was evident in the man's continued presence. The Kid instead of Clell should have been put on his trail. The guy was no more a parson than he, Bates McCartrey, was Geronimo's uncle.

The Straddlebug range boss had good reason to distrust strangers. He had covered his tracks well and fortified his actions with some pretty sharp thinking as a basis for possible alibis, but was not sitting so tight he could afford to take chances. He was far too shrewd to imagine the Government was going to overlook those homestead evictions. Which was why he'd decided to have this filing on Crescent play a strong part in the campaign against Fardel. If there were blame this should tie it right on to Fick's coat tails.

McCartrey, tightening the grip of brawny legs about the horse, grinned into the gathering darkness. It was time to dissociate himself from Fick and Straddlebug. All the groundwork was laid, all his pipelines open. Not for nothing had he put those tough hands on Fick's payroll. Some of the older crew that had never been brought into Bates' scheming were already at work rounding up the McCartrey cattle Fick allowed him to run; he would hire what he could of these away when he quit. Their honesty would be convincing, sponsor for any fabrications he might feed investigating badgetoters. The tough hands would continue, under Fick, to take his orders. The poor dumb bastard, he thought, was just asking for it!

But his good humor trickled away when his remembering mind came to the fellow that town bunch was calling 'Parson.' All the ugliness in him heated up its intolerance as he recalled how the 'parson' had talked by the coach to Pauline that night after helping her out ... the intimate sound of her voice and that handclasp!

McCartrey cursed the fellow roundly. He wasn't ready yet for Government snoopers. He cursed Beaupre, too, for fetching Cherry into it, thinking of the chance the stranger'd had to get his ears filled. No telling what mishmash these fool girls had let fly!

The beating, at least, had kept the man inactive. No matter what he had learned or how much he suspected, the fellow had had little chance to make dangerous use of it ... He would surely not be stupid enough to file a report from Red Post. Before he could file one any place else...

Lips tight, McCartrey nodded and heeled his horse into motion. He'd see Horner tonight. That kill-crazy Kid should be prime; and maybe, while he was at it, something might as well happen to Beaupre.

He put his mind to it, turning the horse deeper into the south to avoid traveled trails until he could cut the homesteaders' camp from some angle that would not leave incriminating tracks. Cherry would keep, this other was urgent. Coming nearer he slowed, pulling into a walk while he took off his gloves and blew on chilled fingers.

But when he got to the camp Joe Walker—nicknamed 'Minus'—was the only one around. McCartrey's eyes showed ugly. 'Where's Horner?' he said, and Walker spat disgustedly. 'Tomcattin'—like he's done every night since we been here.' He turned to brighten the fire but the range boss stopped him. 'Leave be,' he growled; and the man, dropping the wood, rubbed gnarled hands on patched Levi's. 'Got any idea when he will likely be back?'

'Depends on what luck he's had. If he's got hold of a . . .' Walker let that go and said instead, 'I kin tell you one thing. If he gits back early he won't be in no case to argue with.'

'If he gets back,' McCartrey said, 'you tell him to stick right here till I see him. And first thing tomorrow you start puttin' that shack up.'

Yanking his horse round he struck out for Fardel's. He saw the lights of the place half a mile before he reached it and spent that much time getting hold of his temper. He had a part to play here that would take all the skill he could manage; as Fick had observed, the boss of Crescent was no fool.

Crescent headquarters showed the ravages of indifference in a dozen slipshod ways. The corrals, dimly glimpsed in the dapples of light from back windows, looked like a good wind would flatten them; the nearer poles were obviously held up, nester fashion, with haywire. The buildings themselves, though well placed and constructed, showed neglect in sagging doors, in broken windows and runnels where undiverted rain-water had channeled their sides in past storms. The yard was a tangle of ragweed and cockleburrs.

McCartrey, looking around with contempt, was hailed from the trees a few lengths short of the veranda and pulled up, chagrined and startled not to recognise the voice. A vague shape darkly showed behind the cold wink of gun-metal. The voice said, 'W'at you do here, eh?'

The syndicate man, who had no use for Mexicans, growled with an impatient arrogance, 'Where's Fardel?'

In the blackness the man with the gun scuffed his feet and did not speak, until the silence, piled up again, had grown explosive with McCartrey's anger. Even then he remained still until McCartrey, roweling the big horse forward, set it snorting back on its haunches at the click that rasped sharply through the sound of its hoofs.

A laugh came softly from the patchwork of shadows. 'Is good night for die—no?' When he got no answer to this the voice said, 'The grass she will maybe not steal so easy now there is a gun on thees ranch.' The voice roughened. 'My arm grows tired, hombre.'

McCartrey, silently furious, glowered into the threat of that gun barrel. There had been no help on this place two weeks past. 'Come out here,' he growled, 'so I can see who I'm talkin' to.'

'A bullet. An' you will know w'en it kees you, even with the eyes shut. Maybe better you tell w'at I ask, eh? Before the finger sleeps.'

A door skreaked on the veranda. Cherry's voice said out of the gloom, 'Is that you, Bates?'

McCartrey said testily, 'Who else did you think would be comin' around? Call off your dog before he gets himself kicked.'

He could not make her out in the darkness obscuring the front of the house. Funny, he thought, that all the light was in back. It made him suddenly less sure of himself, strangely uneasy and reluctant to get down, even when she said, 'It's all right, Tony,' as though, once aground, he might find himself trapped.

'Come in, Bates,' she said. 'I'll go make a light for you.'

He followed her in, glad to get out of sight of that guy in the cedars. She scratched a match in the living room, and as the wick lifted flame pressed the glass chimney inside its brass prongs. She set the lamp on the mantel and turned to face him, asking quietly, 'Do you think my father will give up without a fight?'

McCartrey smiled and reached for her and when she eluded his arms he said, nettled, 'You don't think I'm backin' that, do you?

104

Hell's fire! I come over here to—' He broke off, observing the differences two weeks had made, taking warning from the way she was watching him.

He pulled in a deep breath. 'To what?' she said flatly.

'That feller outside—where'd he come from?'

'I found him out on the desert, half dead, and took care of him. Do you think I ought to have asked you first?'

'A damn stray,' McCartrey growled, 'and a *cholo* at that. Well, no matter,' he said, getting hold of himself. 'Might turn out a good thing you done it. Where's Fardel?'

Her eyes darkened. 'He's resting.'

McCartrey was too shrewd to sneer except in his mind. The boss of Crescent was always 'resting' in between his bouts with the bottle. 'Put the coffee on while I'm gettin' him up. There's things he's got to know and he better be wide awake when he hears 'em.'

'Things like what?'

McCartrey, twisting big shoulders, discovered the girl's father owlishly from the hall. There was a gun in his fist and, though he had to hang onto the wall to stay upright, his bleary eyes didn't look near as vague as you'd expect.

McCartrey grinned. 'Glad you're up. Was just fixin' to—'

'Get off this ranch and stay off,' Fardel

said, waving the pistol and glaring.

McCartrey, in spite of rising blood pressure, managed to break out a look of astonishment that was almost ludicrous in its paraded suggestion of injured innocence. 'That the way you talk to a man that's rode—'

'You've rode your welcome right off this place—think I don't know what you come sneaking around for? Get back on that bronc and light a shuck out of here.'

The damned old dodo really meant it, Bates saw. He shook the scowl off his face. 'Man that's losin' grass has got a right to paw around some but—Hell's fire, Fardel! I come over here to help you. To warn and tell you how—'

'When I need or take advice from you I'll be a sight farther gone than I am right now. You going to climb on that horse or...'

'We may as well hear him out,' Cherry said.

Fardel, blinking, got his feet braced and scrubbed the hand he took away from the wall across the snuff-streaked hair of his mustache.

'You're a man of education,' McCartrey said. 'Does it stand to reason, things bein' like they are, I'd ride plumb over here just to get myself shot at? Soon's they get up their shack Fick's figurin' to lease your grass from them gunnies; but if you'll listen to what I

106

come here to tell you I'll show you how you can beat this deal.'

'Save your wind,' Fardel sneered.

'By Gawd,' McCartrey said, whipping his glance to the girl, 'does he *want* to lose this place?'

She shook her head. Fardel said, 'I'd sooner lose it fighting with my back to the wall then depend on the word of a man who'd sell his own boss down the river.'

Outrage turned McCartrey's eyes black as jet. He half raised a big fist, then let it fall, swearing. In a half-strangled voice he said, 'I ain't workin' for that ... that *sidewinder* any more—I quit the damn spread! I say, by Gawd, I got a bellyful!' He glanced sideways at the girl. 'I come over here to help you, to throw in with your ol' man; but if he's goin' to get his back up, if he'd rather have that chili-eater for a son-in-law than a white man...'

He paused, still eyeing the girl. Her expression did not change, but now her father said, lowering the pistol, 'Did I understand you to imply you are willing—'

'Willin'!' McCartrey said bitterly, 'I been willin' and urgin' for more'n eight months—she can tell you herself the only reason we ain't hitched is 'cause she won't say the word!'

'Is that so?' Fardel asked, swinging a look at his daughter.

'He's showed willing enough,' she said, watching McCartrey, but there was that in her tone which made her father look puzzled. He scrubbed his mustache again and shoved the gun in his waistband. 'Maybe I spoke out of turn,' he told McCartrey, plainly not satisfied yet prepared to drop it. 'You got something to say, go ahead.'

'We got to fight,' McCartrey growled. 'We got to get those birds out of there. They've filed, but until they've proved up, Fick can't legally put his cows on your grass. He's hell for bein' legal, but he can't wait—he can't afford to with his stock skin and bones and losin' calves every day. He's got to get them cattle onto grass and water.'

'Sounds reasonable,' Fardel nodded. 'What do you propose to do?'

'What about this Mex drifter? He any good with that gun?'

'Suppose,' Cherry said, 'we let him answer that himself.'

Fardel shook his head. 'The man's got no stake in this.'

'All right,' McCartrey said, 'I'll run them off myself,' and saw the girl's watching eyes change. With this token, he said, grinning toughly, 'Guess that shows where *I* stand.'

'Will you move them tonight?'

McCartrey, eyes on the girl, finally nodded.

'I'll have Primero sweep out the

bunkhouse,' said Fardel, producing what was left in his bottle. He held it up to the light and reluctantly extended it.

'When will you be back?'

McCartrey's face pulled into a frown before he swallowed. It had not been any part of his plan to come back this side of the fireworks. But with the girl like she was he knew he'd got to move careful.

'Soon as I can,' he told Fardel, 'though that might not be for a couple of days. I've got things to be done and a bunch of loose stock to be combed from the Straddlebugs. I might have to find—'

'Use our grass. Bring them here,' Cherry said.

McCartrey had no intention of placing his cows in such jeopardy, but he was faced with the need of keeping her mouth shut until his pattern for empire picked up some momentum. Considering the shape of her breasts he felt again the wild hunger explode through his veins—that hunger of wanting which she had never fulfilled and never would of her own intention. She wanted to get out of this country, and talk didn't interest her. She saw through his large promises and now she jarred him again.

'That's what you want to do, ain't it?'

McCartrey's black eyes hid the hate that surged up in him. 'As a matter of fact I've prob'ly got them sold, but if the deal falls through I suppose I might have to. In which case,' he said, 'I will pay for the privilege. Now there's just one more thing,' he told Fardel. 'I'm goin' to move those birds off, but we've no guarantee Fick won't go on with it, anyway. If he does you've got to protect yourself from him until I get back. With guns if you have to.' He picked up his hat.

Cherry said, brushing past him, 'I'll go as far as your horse.'

CHAPTER NINE

Irish, looking into that glowering face, understood he had come to the end of deception. Acting a parson had never been more than a wild hope at best; yet it was hard, bitter hard, to see the chance kicked out from under him by so mean a thing as this unwashed and whiskerless Kid. He sought to find some way round the challenge or of at least postponing the threatened exposure, but his body cringed away from the thought of further punishment and his gambler's pride would not let him seem a coward in front of these people while he had beneath his armpit the means of dealing with Horner as tradition demanded.

Having put the need of security behind, he

found that his mind had grown astonishingly calm. There was anger in him, yes, a juiceless displeasure with the antics of Fate, but there was no longer panic or fright. He could look at this Kid as he could at the predicament he had got himself into, and, knowing both, coldly despise them.

Something of this may have got through to the fellow. He let go of Bert's arm and backed off a step, staring. Complete silence enveloped them; not a man in the crowd moved so much as a finger. Horner's breath came as though he'd been running. Someone gasped when the preacher said, 'Get on with it, boy—what you waiting for?'

Horner's gray, pinched face was stiff with hate. He found himself in the position of having engineered something he was unable to finish. His self-respect was being ground into the dirt. He knew what they'd be telling behind his back and his outraged ego demanded instant retribution. There was murder in his heart but no response in his muscles. He could not have moved his hand an inch for all the undug gold in the country.

There was nothing of danger in the parson's stance, nothing frightening at all about the man's reputation. Clell, it was said, had half beaten his head off. His face was still bandaged, yet Horner couldn't move. It was what he read in those gray eyes that stopped him.

111

Time stood still. He felt pressure build in him until, unable to face the man longer, he wheeled with a cry of frustrated fury and plunged through the crowd to become lost in the night.

Irish's stare flicked across the shocked faces that in these deep shadows looked like blobs of pale dough. Without comment he moved through the lane silently opened, to stop in remembrance as his boots reached the walk. He turned round and came back, got into the buckboard and picked up the reins and drove the team to the livery. He tossed some silver at the night boss and went on to the hotel.

In his rooms he considered his face in the cracked mirror. Tomorrow the doc was to have peeled off those rags.

He could not wait for tomorrow. The time to get out of this country was now, before the saloon man or Fick's range boss made some further move. A vision of Pauline Fick crossed his mind. She would be expecting him at Bessingers'...

He turned out the lamp and raised a window that looked down on Beaupre's roof and the alley that ran between this place and the saloon. He studied the murky slot of its passage. There was a door, he remembered, giving into a card room behind Beaupre's bar, but the likelihood of this being opened seemed too remote to distract his thinking.

He relit the lamp and took it over to the washstand. Gingerly removing the dressings from his face, he considered what the mirror showed him. With a towel dabbed into the chipped crockery pitcher he cleansed his face and regarded it again. The shape of his nose was indubitably changed, and the scabbed-over gash in his cheek would not be mentioned in any of the descriptions put out for him. He spent an irritable while picking out the stitches and an additional ten minutes impatiently couched in a chair trying to rid himself of accumulated tension.

When his thoughts began to intrude on this process he snuffed the lamp and went back to the window, discarding the notion of depending on sheets. Such a device would get him down safely, but the last thing he wanted was to advertise his flight. The longer this town was kept in ignorance of it the better his chance.

It seemed a pretty slim prospect any way you considered it.

He climbed over the sill and hanging on by his fingers despite the pain to his ribs let himself down until he judged his boots were not ten feet above ground.

The fall jarred but did not tumble him. He turned at once through the gloom, and, feeling his way towards the rear, was just abreast of the door into Beaupre's private card room when the rasp of a latch struck through the conglomerate of wall-muted noises. Irish instinctively crouched to wheel into a run; then his mind, overhauling the impulse, snatched him back to press broad shoulders flat against the wall.

The door was pulled open. Light streamed past the emerging man's shape, limning a grotesque shadow against the hotel wall. There was a mumble of voices, the man calling back over a shoulder, 'The hell with you!' The door was banged shut and the man, cursing as he tried to pick his way through the blackness, stumbled away towards the street.

Irish let go of his held breath. At the alley's back end he paused briefly beyond the buildings to scan the roundabout shadows. These back lots were less dark than he had hoped and expected. Twin shafts of light from the hotel kitchen's back windows, cutting into the murk, disclosed a litter of cans and broken crates strewn over the ground where the cook had heaved them. To reach the livery from here he'd have to cross that glare, and his plan to take one of the team he had left there, as though for Pauline, did not seem as convenient or wise as he'd imagined.

He didn't have much choice. No other horses were available unless he helped himself from the Palace hitch-rack. Taking another deep breath, and mindful of the clarity of outside sounds at night, he crossed the light from the windows and did not lower his hackles until he came, across lots, to the stables. The night man said, 'Well, she goin' home after all?'

'Couldn't say,' Irish told him. 'I've come by for that horse I had out the other day.'

He observed the man covertly scrutinizing his face and stepped back against a partition out of sight from the lantern-lit entrance, apparently deep in thought, while the fellow fetched the animal—a big dun—and with the skill of long practice slipped a bridle over its head. The horse tongued the bit. The night boss said, 'May come on to git right down brisk before mornin',' with his glance shifting over the parson's thin coat. Irish let it go. When the horse stood ready he swung up and took the reins. The man said, 'Hear you put on quite a show this evenin',' and Irish fretfully asked which was the best way to Crescent.

'Just strike out west with the stage road till you git to the foothills. Keep your eyes to the right after you pass Pilot Knob. You likely been past goin' out to that buryin'. Watch for three red-barked pines and turn north. About another eight mile back into the place. You won't hev no trouble,' he said, stepping aside.

Irish would have liked mighty well to be sure of that. He was in a lather to get away from here but held the horse down to a walk through the lane, seeing behind the dingy glass of O'Dowd's several shirt-sleeved men grouped about a green-topped table, one fellow vigorously chalking his cue. None of the faces registered, barely touching the edge of his attention, most of which was given over to keeping his mount in the deepest shadows.

The stage station was dark, the eastbound having gone through the town yesterday and the westbound out of Tucson not due through till tomorrow night. His thoughts remembered the marshal who had been with himself and Fick's daughter coming in and he wondered again what had taken him to Sells. Hadn't he said they weren't having Indian troubles out this way?

Irish reached inside his coat, averting his face as the horse passed the Palace, damply fingering the grip of his pistol; but no one came out and nobody hailed. There was something going on up ahead, he discovered when he fetched his attention back again to the front. He saw a bobble of lights and a huddle of men bunched about a large wagon—quite a crowd by the look.

This was beyond the town limits, and as Irish came nearer he made out the vehicle to be some manner of freight outfit, its canvas stretched over bows like the rig of a Conestoga. He'd seen a number of these derelicts of the westward migration and had always felt the motive power had been given insufficient recognition in the achievement. There were oxen corralled beyond the masted tongue of this one and a man stood in front of it repeatedly holding aloft for inspection something that reflected the light from the lanterns as he harangued the jostling multitude.

Irish felt that discretion made it wise to avoid them and reined the dun off the road where he could skirt the illumination with less chance of its footfalls attracting their notice. He caught brief portions of the oratory and remembered the Ophir biscuit-shooter's reference to a 'medicine man.' The visiting celebrity may not have had a golden tongue but he had a stock of phrases designed to put gold into his pockets.

'... And nowhere, friends, *no*where will you find any other medicinal with the curative properties of this one! Tanguitari Snake Oil is guaranteed—and I repeat, *guaranteed*—to relieve every pain in your body within a period of ten days or I'll return to you every dime you've invested—every penny! Nor is that all! If you are not completely satisfied with the results within one week...'

Across this distance—even in the lantern's shine—Irish, unable to make out the man's features, judged him to be garbed in the popular conception of scout or trapper. His hair was worn as long as a squaw man's and held, by the look of it, the same greasy gleam. Irish, wasting scant thought on him, angled back to the road as soon as his words became unintelligible, holding the dun closely in hand a while longer before letting it have the all-out run it had been crowding for.

After a fast quarter-mile of this he pulled the animal into a lope, trailing the stage road west until the saw-toothed rim of the Comobabis cut blackly across the glittering wink of the stars. He stopped the horse then with his head turned, listening.

Apparently his departure had not yet been discovered by any agents of McCartrey or others who might have an unhealthy interest in his whereabouts. Irish thought of Clell and Beaupre particularly, but the saloon-keeper would hardly seek him out during business hours without his plans called for sudden use of the reverend influence. And should this be the case he would assume, when he connected with the stableman, that Irish had gone to Fardel's ranch. Which was why Bert had asked directions.

He had no intention of visiting Crescent. Neither Cherry's note nor his deductions about her could sway the urgent need he felt for piling up distance between himself and this Basin—all the distance he could and as quickly as possible. Despite the enumerated choices of direction the marshal had given him Irish knew there was but one affording chance of ultimate victory. He would have to swing north through the mountains. Somewhere this side of discovery and Gu Achi—one of the small Indian settlements—he had got to twist south again or permanently disappear.

The glowering face of 'that horrible Kid' suddenly burst through his thinking and premonition drove bleak talons coldly into his quivering attention.

This escape would have to be thorough. No longer was it going to be enough to elude the Governor's star-packers; it would not even be sufficient now to get himself over the line into Mexico. He realized, bitterly hating it, that while such a course might defeat the law it would prove no hindrance at all to the Kid.

Irish had made an implacable enemy. He had made the mistake of scaring a snake he should have taken his gun to right on the spot. He had made the fellow appear trifling and ridiculous in front of people who had held him in deadliest fear. Horner would not forget this. He would never again be able to hold up his head until by his own hands he had destroyed the man who had so cavalierly outfaced and ignored him.

It was a terrible thought, but Irish knew in

his bones it was a correct evaluation of what he could now look for. Flight in itself could no longer serve. He would find no security while Horner lived.

Unless he could trick the Kid into believing he had accomplished what he most certainly would try to accomplish, Bert Irish and his identity as Red Post parson must cease to exist and be wiped from men's minds or he would die in truth. He saw this vividly. So real did it become for him that he half swung the gelding round in its tracks, thinking to go back and have it out with Horner. What stopped him was the conviction the Kid would not face him and the knowledge that he, Bert Irish, could not kill in cold blood.

With a curse he spun the horse about and drove it furiously on, impatient to get into the cover of the mountains where at least he would be able to get rid of his tracks. He wasn't fooled into thinking this would throw the Kid off; at best it might allow him to stage his own 'finish.' Otherwise Horner would bide his time and, when it suited him, strike from ambush.

But as the deeper dark of the foothills closed round him, Bert, reconsidering, came to believe it would be better to pull the man into Mexico. There he could devote full attention to Horner; here he'd have to dodge both him and the law.

He knew from the sheriff's talk aboard stage that Haines had spread his Indians with muzzle-loaders across the desert between San Miguel and some point south of Ruby, a mining camp in the Sierraitas considerably east and a bit north of Osa. This was why Bert had figured to push north now through the rock-ribbed canyons of the Comobabis. Another desert lay beyond and, after it, still other mountains. Crossing these he could continue west, heading for Baja California. Or, turning due south in the vicinity of Ajo, he could try again to cross the line into Mexico. If he recruited every Papago on the Reservation Haines could not patrol the entire border.

Nor did Irish think it likely the border authorities would be overly vigilant now that some of the pressure had worn off. Border authorities were human too; they'd not be anxious to do any more work than they had to.

This was the ticket, Irish thought. Go north and let his trail play out in those canyons, perhaps leaving some of his clothes or other means of identification alongside a few bones if he happened to find any. Then take off for Mexico and hope for the best.

He settled down to his riding, not pushing the horse now, but keeping it moving, hunting a place where he could leave the road without this becoming too plainly apparent. It would be risky, of course, for he might wind up in some damned box canyon; but the night was filled with risk and nothing could be worse right now than to fall into the hands of those gun-packing Papagos.

He breathed a sigh of deep thanks that they were far to the south of him; the last thing he needed at this point was Indian trouble. A picture of Pauline stole into his mind and surprised him with its clarity ... He regretted having to leave without some parting word. Cherry Fardel was attractive with her needs and taut compulsions, but Irish had known her kind in half a hundred places. He had never known anyone quite like Pauline Fick with her queer slanting eyes and the feeling of breathlessness her proximity inspired.

He could not accurately place the true source of what she held for him or the excitement he'd so strongly felt while holding her hand by the stage that time. Perhaps in her reality she represented the substance of all the dreams that had gotten away from him, the good things in life that he had never got hold of, that always seemed when he reached to slide away through his fingers. One thing he was sure of—she called up the best in him.

He was topping the second ridge—knob, in the stableman's language—when he became aware of a lesser darkness to the left of him; not exactly a glow, for there were no clouds to reflect it, but definitely a something between sky and earth that was lighter, a kind of haze like mist or the far-off gleam of snow. Not a small thing nor a tall one, more like a shimmer of foxfire extending south from a little behind him in a kind of loose half-moon clear to a point on his north-west right.

More out of curiosity than with any definite sense of alarm he reined the horse sharply left off the road where the ground, inclining upwards towards a bald and slanting outcrop, seemed to promise a larger view.

Skirting blurred patches of wind-bent oak he noticed the pungence of pine, the feathery odor of dust and a whir of dead leaves fluttering past in the draught. A disturbed bird squawked as it went flapping away and his glance raked that direction before, with a shrug, he stepped out of the saddle, securing the reins with a twist to a tree. The rock felt rough and treacherous under his feet and it proved more of a climb than he'd supposed it would be. He stopped in his tracks with his jaws locked tight as his glance cleared the ledge and he saw what lay yonder.

CHAPTER TEN

He had thought of fire and impatiently dismissed it—for where would there be grass to burn with none available save Fardel's to the north of him? This wind was blowing right out of the north and carried no slightest taint of smoke.

It was fire just the same, though no grass was responsible. Winking pinpoints of light stretched across the desert floor like a necklace of jewels carelessly dropped on black velvet. In a great half-circle this gleaming chain hemmed the roundabout hills. To the south and west the watch-fires glowed and deep into the north along the hills' farther sides.

No one had to tell Irish what this meant. While he crouched there, scowling, he understood what had sent that bird off its roost and why he had smelled that lifted dust. He caught, quite unmistakably, the sound of a traveling horse.

The skin of his back twitched and tingled, but he remained where he was until he knew beyond question the man was angling down through some pass to the west of here. He moved then, swiftly clambering back to his horse, jerking loose the reins and throwing his leg across leather.

He whirled the dun, driving it down-slope headlong, determined to intercept that rider, unwarrantably convinced there must be some connection between this fellow and that business below. Another hunch, perhaps?—Bert knew only he must get to the road before this horseman got by.

He made it, trusting the howl of the wind to screen his racket. He wanted the man to know he was coming from town, and he was in the road, pointed west, when the fellow materialized out of the shadows. Bert saw the lift of a gun as the man swerved his horse, abruptly blocking the way. 'Stay where you're at! Give your name! State your business!'

The sharp demands stiffened Irish. He said, suddenly cool, 'If this is a hold-up you're wasting your time.'

'Strike a light,' the other growled. 'I want a look at your mug.'

The match lived about as long as Bert had expected in this gale, but recognition was mutual. 'The parson!' Haines swore. 'What's happened to your face an' what're you doin' up here at this hour?'

'Heading for Crescent,' Irish said, 'and the face is what you can expect in my business.'

The sheriff laughed. 'You take it well. Who worked you over?'

'A hard man to convince. Name of Clell, I believe.'

'He's a rough one,' Haines nodded, pushing his gun back in leather. 'So you're bound for Crescent. How is the old goat?'

'About as usual, I imagine. Did you get your man?'

'No, but I will. He never slipped over the border, that's sure. We're handlin' this like a rabbit kill. We're comin' up all around here. Got fires strung out all over the desert and half the Reservation standin' ready between 'em. I got deputies swingin' down from the north and another crew closin' in from the east. We'll git the bugger,' he told Irish confidently.

'If he were around here,' Bert said, 'it seems likely your Indians would have discovered him by this time—found his trail anyway. I expect you've seen the last of him.'

'Don't you believe it! Just because he ain't gone into the barrens ain't no good reason for thinkin' he's swung back again. Fact of the matter is he can't *git* back! I took your hunch an' had the two sheriffs north of here put out patrols. He's holed up, that's where he is—an' I'll smoke him out if I hev to swear ever' man in this county!'

*　　　*　　　*

It was crowding ten by the time Irish sighted Crescent's buildings. He'd neither intended nor wanted to come here but his meeting

126

with the sheriff had left him little choice. With this whole end of Arizona swarming with bounty hunters, many of whom would doubtless shoot on sight, any man knowing the region no better than Bert would be a plumb fool to try and get through.

He'd better hole up here at Crescent where there was someone to vouch for him, as Cherry would, than attempt to do anything else right at present. That sheriff was determined, and nothing, for a while at least, was going to persuade him to abandon that reward money.

Irish's talk about trouble between Crescent and Straddlebug had, as Bert's father would have phrased it, fallen on stony ground. It had caught even less than the edge of Haines' attention. 'Later,' he'd said irritably to Bert's suggestion that he go out there. When Irish, persisting as an actual parson might, had continued to fill in the picture with all the disturbing ugliness inherent in syndicate aggression, the sheriff had hauled off and declared with snarling intolerance he wasn't mixing in no damn range feud and what happened to 'them fool cowmen' was the Government's concern; that he wasn't about to see no dough like that trickle through his fingers to go slamming after an outfit controlling as many election votes as the Santa Cruz Land & Cattle Company. No matter what any whey-faced sky pilot though of it!

Which was about as much benefit as Irish could hope for. Now, at least, he could feel reasonably confident he had insulated the sheriff from any likelihood of visiting Fardel's.

*　　*　　*

McCartrey, striking south-east through the night in the direction of the camp he had already visited, had his back humped like a mule in a hailstorm. Nothing had gone quite the way he had planned it. The girl had her head filled with foolishness about that 'preacher,' and anyone other than Beaupre would have had better sense than to have brought them together. Beaupre never ought to have been figured in this deal! Bad as he'd needed those farmers to get things started...

McCartrey cursed in a passion. He could have found other ways—that slick-talking dive-keeper had boggled his lines at every turn and the way it looked now he had done it deliberate; the double-crosser never had intended to play McCartrey's game; he had been purely out to feather his nest and use McCartrey both ends from the middle.

The range boss, fuming, raked his mount with the steel. No use stewing about that now—Kid could take care of him when he went after that snoop of a parson. Fardel, anyways, had finally shown a little sense.

One thing a man could count on—Fardel's stubbornness. For all the man's drunken shiftlessness he would never knowingly permit himself to be shoved out of this hand-built oasis. When it came to a question of survival he would fight; and now that he thought Bates McCartrey was back of him he'd swell up like a carbuncle at the first sight of syndicate cattle. He'd remember Bates' warning and heat up that rifle.

The game, regardless, was in Bates' hands. He hadn't aimed to get mixed up in this directly, had planned to egg the old man into tangling with Fick's filers. Maybe this way was better. When you wanted a thing done right you generally got farther when you did it yourself.

The more he turned it over the better McCartrey liked the whole set-up. Unless the Kid had come back there'd be no one at camp but old Walker. Everybody knew Walker. He'd come in with that plague of sodbusters, and the only reason he was still in the country was because, at the time, no one had happened to lay eyes on him. When the rest of the farmers had been moved off their places Walker had been in the barber's tub fighting off an attack of two-headed pink elephants. Hadn't seemed much point after that in bothering him. He had let his hundred and forty go and come whining out to the ranch to see Fick, and the chicken-hearted slob, to ease his own conscience, had put Walker on as chore-boy. There wasn't one living soul this side of the mountains...

Walker was asleep, stinking of forty-rod and snoring, when McCartrey found his dying fire. The range boss canvassed the surroundings with a pair of contemptuous eyes and was about to get out of the saddle when he thought better of it. The man's staked-out horse whickered tentative greetings. Bates cuffed his own before it could widen trembling nostrils, afterwards kneeing it around through the shadows till he was satisfied the Kid had not returned yet from his unauthorised prowling.

McCartrey let out a banshee yell that should have brought Walker out of his blankets. When it didn't he took down his rope, popping the end of it at Walker's legs until the old man, spluttering curses, struggled up on an elbow to peer blearily around. When he became sufficiently collected to focus McCartrey and stumble whiningly to his feet the range boss said, with the rope's end dangling from his pointing left fist: 'What the hell did you let that critter in here for?'

Walker swung round to see what he was pointing at and the gun in McCartrey's right hand spat flame.

McCartrey's lips curled as he strapped the coiled rope back onto his saddle. The weedbender's horse, tied slipshod as usual, had taken off in a panic, which was all right with Bates. He turned his own and rode off, comfortably convinced that when the Kid got back and made out what had happened things were going to shape up just about the way he wanted them.

★   ★   ★

Cherry, after McCartrey's mounted shape had gone loping off into the black mass of the night, turned back towards the sagging grey planks of the veranda still at war with the unresolved tensions inside her. The man was virile, even dangerously attractive in his undisciplined, arrogant, challenging way; but she knew McCartrey well enough to be convinced in her own mind he would never be the answer to the need that ever more surely, more remorselessly was pushing her towards the brink of something which might prove to be disaster.

It was not dislike of the man or distrust which had bitterly kept her from responding but the knowledge that his roots were here, that he never would consider pulling out of this bleak country.

Cherry hated the Basin with every fiber of her being. All her nineteen years had been

131

spent in this environment and she felt ready to scream every time she looked around her. What was the use of being alive in a place where nothing ever changed or ever happened?—where each hour of each day of every week was repetition?—where over and over and over again it was the same homely tasks, the same monotonous faces? Where each tick of the clock watched the fullness of youth irrevocably trudging farther down the trail of vanished yesterdays?

She was filled with an explosive recklessness which she knew every male in the country had sensed, which more than a few had attempted to tap with their hangdog grins and half-furtive advances. But Cherry wanted more, a lot more, than swapping one side of this picture for the other. She wanted an end to this insufferable dreariness, to get caught up in a whirl of new sounds and strange people where life could be seized and sampled and felt.

'Thees man,' the Mexican said, coming up, 'is no good for you. No good for nothing.'

She looked around in the butter-yellow shaft from the door and saw how the light fell across his blunt cheekbones, the wayward curl of black hair that darkly shadowed his forehead below the saucerlike brim of his chin-strapped sombrero. He was young enough to be aware of her moods, to understand what she'd been thinking and allow his reactions to get into the tone of voice which repeated, 'No good!' like a curse before he stepped back to get his face into shadow.

She recalled where and how she had found him, knew he worshipped the ground she walked on in the unshakable partisan way of his race—that he would kill for her if he had to. He understood what she had, what she could bring to a man, and his regard, she could see, put a high value on it; but he knew too well his own place in this country. He would die for her, yes, but his obligation stood between them and was a barrier he'd never cross.

Turning away she went into the house, pushing the door shut with the backs of her shoulders and standing there with her unbearable tension, feeling like pounding herself insensible against it. She had never met Jack Horner, but she had seen the Kid and heard the wild tales that linked his name with murder. She thought of him now with her terrible need and half turned to go out and catch up a horse before remembering that this was where McCartrey was bound for, that long before she could get there he would have run the man off.

No, she thought with a bitter shake of the head, Bates would not run him off; Bates would make a deal with him. She had no illusions about Bates McCartrey.

She was reaching for the lamp to blow it out when she caught hoof sound. She stood listening with hand still lifted and heard the horse come on, not fast but rather aimlessly walking as though its rider were of two minds about his course. An unconscionable time appeared to be consumed before Primero's gruff challenge drove through the sound and stopped it.

Cherry stood without breathing, trying to catch the man's words, but they were pitched too low for her to make out what he was saying.

Primero said, 'I do not know you. Turn around the *caballo*—'

'Ask the girl. She's been taking care of me.'

Cherry's mind whirled. She felt weak in the knees. Then she flung open the door and ran onto the veranda. 'It's all right—it's all right! Take care of his horse.' She flew down the steps. 'You'll stay the night, won't you, Parson?'

'You got room in that bunkhouse?'

'Of course!' She laughed shakily. 'Pap'll bust if he don't see you!' She scuffed her feet. 'Come on—get down! Have you et?' she cried as he creaked out of the saddle. 'Coffee's on the back of the stove and it won't take but a shake—'

'In the morning, thanks,' Bert Irish said,

and followed his horse and Primero across the yard.

CHAPTER ELEVEN

Irish heard the skreak of the Mexican's bunk ropes before the day had yet begun to grow light. Snuggling deeper into scratchy blankets he heard the man get into his spur-jangling boots, shiveringly pull on his pants and go out to take care of whatever it was he had got himself up for. His prowling thoughts touched the girl and her disappointment last night at his evasion of the trap she'd tried to build with that talk of coffee.

He turned over, sighing as he resettled the blankets, and thought a long while about his personal prospects, which didn't look any better for the sleep he'd put on them.

This was a bad situation he had stepped into here. When Fick made his play to grab this range there was going to be trouble; and that kill-crazy Kid was on the Straddlebug payroll. Against these facts, however, reconsideration of the chances convinced him, as it had last night, there was no place else he could go without running into the reward-hungry guns of Haines' posse. Not even in town could he hope to avoid this.

135

The noose of steel was tightening and in town there was Beaupre blandly smiling his threat of going to the sheriff.

He tried to haze his thoughts towards Pauline but was able only to evoke the nagging recollection of the night he'd stood with her hand in his beside the coach under the station overhang. He couldn't bring her back, and it turned him bitterly moody to discover how clearly he could recapture in all its changing shades of expression the gold-framed face of Fardel's daughter.

His mind felt threadbare with the churn of all this thinking, the continuing run of his thoughts too filled with depression and the dregs of self-knowledge to permit of further shelving in sleep. His head was full of strange fancies, like the distortion of images glimpsed in a cheap mirror, and he was against the rough edge of things he could touch but not identify. In this mood the two girls became symbols of his lifelong struggle between the forces of good and evil, between the easy way and the hard road of virtue. Cherry he could see with the sharpest clarity... Cherry whom Beaupre had fetched to take care of him... Cherry holding herself out to him with all that there was of her.

*   *   *

From the business of Walker, McCartrey,

bound for Straddlebug, stopped off in town long enough to pass the word that he had broken with Fick and left the syndicate's employ. He made it seem this talk was dragged out of him, coloring his account to fasten all blame for what was building on the herringboned shoulders of the syndicate's resident manager. 'I warned Fick time and again he was overstockin'—I told him we was in for this drought and he laughed at me. I ain't tryin' to set myself up for no lily—I done a heap of things on his order that by Gawd went against the grain; but when he come out with this deal for puttin' the skids under that old man I told him to give me my time!'

It was in the Palace with the crowd standing six deep around him that McCartrey did most of his talking, pounding the bar like it was Fick he was walloping and waving his outrage like a bullfighter working for both ears and the tail. He looked fed up with dirty dealing, and when pressed, as he had known he would be, for additional and definite details he clammed up as though suddenly mindful of the obligations due to long employment.

But he let them drag it out of him, spilling the most of his liquor on the floor and bar and some of it even down the hairy front of his half-exposed chest. Despite appearances he was perfectly sober, cunningly calculating even at his blaspheming loudest every word, look and gesture for the effect it would provoke if later recounted before a jury. He was out to damn Fick and the man's Chicago owners and did a very able job of it, finally going so far as to describe the actual mechanics by which the syndicate proposed to liquidate the Fardel holdings.

Leaving the Palace in a hubbub he set out to locate Clell, but failed completely in this effort, running into Horner as he came back to pick up his horse. The gun-handy Kid appeared to be in a difficult mood. McCartrey did not bring up his truancy, but, beckoning him off the road for greater privacy, passed him a roll of bills and said there would be double that much again if the parson turned up with a hole through his skull in a way that also eliminated Beaupre.

The Kid, grunting, pocketed the banknotes without remark, and McCartrey, dropping off his horse at the livery, walked around to the hotel and got a room and went to bed.

*   *   *

In her room at the Bessingers' after the family had retired, Pauline Fick, having tried in vain to sleep, at last got up and, raising its chimney, touched a match to the wick of the lamp. She pulled down the window and drew the shade, slipped a wrap over the ivory gleam of her shoulders and settled into a chair with a copy of *Harper's*.

But her eyes kept wandering from the meaningless print, prowling over the room among things made familiar through previous visits. She couldn't stop the whirl of her thoughts, she was too worked up from those harrowing moments behind the runaway team and what little she had personally observed of that exchange between Horner and the broad-shouldered parson. She had not seen a great deal—Haskins had hurried her away much too quickly—but there had been no shots or other evidence of violence which might have kept the parson away.

This country had changed. She'd never seen the range so dry and bare, or so much dust hanging over everything. But the change went deeper than this—it was in the people, in their uncomfortable silences, in guarded looks and wooden faces. Where was all the laughter she remembered?

Even the Bessingers, though they'd been cordial enough about the table, had seemed to run conversationally thin as they sat round the fire in the living-room later; there had been a marked absence of ordinary gossip. They had asked about her life at school, Grace had inquired about fashions and Tom had half-heartedly attempted to tease about beaux, but they hadn't either of them seemed to be very much concerned; it was as though underneath this conventional politeness they'd been deeply preoccupied with more personal matters. She'd been glad after a while to seize on Tom's yawn to escape to her room.

What was the matter with everybody? Even Haskins, who had seen her through measles and chickenpox, had seemed a little uncomfortable under his fussiness, almost relieved to get away from her. And her father, tonight, had hardly been mentioned. She found this disturbing, recalling the way he had aged these past months. Tom and her dad had always done a lot of hunting, packing into the Mexican mountains together; when she'd asked, Tom had said they hadn't seen much of him. 'What—no cards?' she had laughed. Tom, staring down at his folded hands, had finally remarked that he guessed the long drought was not conducive to card playing.

The parson, too, had seemed a little withdrawn when she had mentioned her father. And he had not come to call.

She had been expecting any moment to hear his step on the porch, had really been looking forward to it, and his failure to appear had probably had as much as anything to do with the dreariness of the evening.

She remembered the way he had held onto her hand that night after helping her off the stage, and, remembering, was able for a little to recapture some of the excitement and wonder she had felt as they had stood there silently considering one another. No other man had ever affected her so ... not even Bates McCartrey.

Last summer she had imagined herself in love with McCartrey, but now she knew she'd been in love with love. Those long winter months in the Old Dominion had disillusioned her, and his failure to write seemed a surer indication of the depth of his own feelings than all his tailored protestations. She understood he'd been amusing himself—gossip has a way of bridging all distance; and her cheeks burned as she recalled his passionate words and inclement kisses.

In the light of the parson's deportment what she'd had from Bates seemed cheap and shoddy. Armed with this new awareness she could not help but suspect what his real goal had been and she did not intend to be alone with him again.

She could not doubt the parson's interest. He had made no declaration—but how could he on such short notice! They had seen each other exactly twice; that time coming in on the stage and then again this evening, when, at the risk of his life, he had so effectively stopped those frightened horses. But she knew deep inside—intuition told her—that what she had felt when he held her hand he had experienced too.

Then why hadn't he come to pay his respects and meet the Bessingers? This was what had so upset the evening. Why, if he cared, had he stayed away?

There might, she thought practically, be a number of reasons—but *what* reasons? Had he been hurt? Had he been called out of town? Had some duty of the cloth proved more important than... But there was nothing more important than complete understanding between a man and a woman—how could there be? That was everything. The two of them together for all time.

She was still thinking about this as she put out the lamp and reopened the window. A moment of wonder that they would find and keep for ever.

She threw off her wrap and got back into bed and felt the tightness of her doubts dissolve as she hugged this good thought to her. Tomorrow everything would look better. Tomorrow she would talk with him again. Perhaps he would ask to ride home with her, or, if he did not, she could suggest it.

*   *   *

She knew when she got up it was going to be a fine day. Yesterday's wind was gone; it was bright and clear with the promise of summer, and outside her window the black-masked sparrows were playing and a cowbird was singing on the handle of the pump. Over breakfast she told Grace she meant to poke around for a while and spend some time hunting yard goods and maybe look through some dress patterns if the Emporium had any new ones.

The older woman smiled. 'Would you like me to go with you?'

'Of course,' Pauline said; but Tom, eyeing her sideways, said to Grace, 'You promised Kathy Benrow you would help with her quilt today,' and Grace, making a face at him, sighed, 'So I did—I guess I'll have to.'

'You go ahead,' Pauline told her. 'I'll probably be going home before the morning's over anyway. I've got to pick up some things the cook has run out of...'

She didn't see the parson that morning. She didn't see Horner either, and for that, at least, she was grateful. At noon she ate lunch at the Ophir and, not finding the parson there, went along to the hotel. The clerk hadn't seen him since he'd gone up last night. 'I don't know where he's got to—never slept in his bed, I kin tell you that much. Mister Beaupre was huntin' him...'

At the livery, which she tried next, the day man said, 'I ain't seen him, ma'am, but he was here last night an' took out that big dun geldin' he favors. Horse ain't back yet.'

Disappointed, she asked him to hitch up the team. But when the outfit was ready she unaccountably changed her mind. The prospect of driving all that weary way alone was suddenly intolerable. She told him to put up the team and get her a saddler. One of the boys could come in later to fetch home the buckboard along with the supplies she had ordered for the cook.

She left town about two on a flax-maned sorrel that had not, the day boss said, been out of the pen for a week. The horse revealed all the evidence of feeling his oats, and, in view of her recent experience, she doggedly held him down to a dissatisfied walk till he quit champing the bit and stopped shaking his head. She let him out a little then but kept a close watch, ready to curb any tendency towards bolting.

Still following the stage road east, two hours later, and with the blue crags of the Roskruge Mountains looming clearer and nearer, she discovered another rider negotiating the crest of one of the hogbacks lifting south of the road. He was perhaps three-quarters of a mile away, traveling in the same direction she was going, hips and upper body starkly limned above the greasewood. She watched him climb onto the skyline, still maintaining his hundred-yard lead. A frown came between her eyes as she watched, and she was starting to bend forward to put that sorrel into a quicker pace when, abruptly stopping, the rider looked back across his shoulder and saw her.

In this thin dry air recognition was mutual. The man was McCartrey. Cold fingers clamped round the girl's heart as he brought the horse about and started down the slope towards her. He was between her and the ranch and there was no way for Pauline to get past him. As he dropped from sight into the bottom of the gully she spun the sorrel, suddenly frantic, and put him into a headlong run.

CHAPTER TWELVE

Beaupre rose at noon, put together a lunch from the stuff on his bar and considered the spectacle staged last night by McCartrey. Done with his snack, he took a cigar from the box standing open in the gleam of the back bar mirror, carefully bit off the end and fired up, puffing thoughtfully.

He had not been on hand during McCartrey's visit, having been at that time trying to locate Bert Irish, who he felt sure was the fellow masquerading as a parson.

Well, Irish—or whatever the man's real name was—would keep. While it was annoying to be put off this way, so long as the fellow had gone to Fardel's he was satisfied. Pursuit of the girl would hold Irish around for as long as Beaupre needed him, and threat of exposure would keep him amenable.

But McCartrey was a different breed of cat entirely. That play, dissociating himself from Fick and Straddlebug, rang its bell of definite warning deep inside the Palace's proprietor. According to the talk McCartrey had been plastered and bitterly blowing off steam. Beaupre knew better. Straddlebug's range boss didn't run off at the mouth; when he said anything it was said for a purpose, and McCartrey on a bender always wound up at Sleazy Annie's. He hadn't gone near the place.

Beaupre had talked with his night shift, and Spots, in command of things behind the bar, had confirmed his suspicions. 'There was plenty of forty-rod flowin', all right, but most of McCartrey's went on the floor.'

Beaupre counted the cash and locked up the surplus in his cast-iron safe. Going around to his desk he dropped into the swivel and, sliding out a drawer, anchored his boot heels and stared through whirls of blue cigar smoke at the ceiling.

146

McCartrey had been inspired by a pair of obvious needs and intentions. To disclaim publicly any further connection with the syndicate and to leave on Fick's doorstep all the blame for whatever came out of this. A man didn't need any rangefinder to understand where the next rock was going to land. Unless Anton Beaupre did some very fast stepping he was liable to find himself laid out in one of Doc's nickel-trimmed caskets.

McCartrey was ready to take off his gloves. According to the plans Beaupre had shared up to this point, the next sound folks heard would be the opening guns of a range feud, fired of necessity by someone at Crescent. The violence had to come from Crescent because the picture they had built up of Fick was too sly and too cautious, too legally sanctimonious, to be caught out on the limb of open aggression.

Fardel was a natural, long groomed for fall guy in the syndicate's supposed plan for empire. Fardel had the water and the grass and bull-moose stubbornness; moreover he stood alone, an obvious target, little better than a squatter. None would doubt he had fired first shot, for he had plainly to fight or see himself done out of his range and the lake which was key to all this lush pasturage. That lake was his pride, and everybody knew it; sole fruit of his education. No one doubted he would defend it. No one but

Beaupre, who'd been party to all the maneuverings.

Beaupre had foreseen McCartrey's reactions when he'd crossed the man up by preventing the murder of Irish. He'd had no hunch at that time of the man's real identity. He had saved him, needing an ace in the hole, against the day when McCartrey, done with sharing, should inevitably attempt to rid himself of a partner he had no more use for. Beaupre, by interfering, had merely hastened the day's arrival.

And now it was here. McCartrey was calling for the discard. He stood ready to step into the shambles of this feud and come out with whatever he could get his damned hooks on. He might not kill his own snakes but they'd be dead just the same; his gunhawk even this minute might be prowling the byways, licking his chops, with a finger curled about the squeeze of his trigger.

Beaupre first. Then Irish—no, that would be going at it wrong. Be the other way around. He would think of the 'parson' as being the more dangerous, assuming—as he'd be bound to—Irish an undercover marshal. It was now, while the deal was in progress, that the proximity of a Federal marshal would have the power to start the sweat in McCartrey—not after the thing was done with.

Beaupre considered warning Irish, but

decided he owed the man nothing. Let him take his chances. Besides, even to attempt such a thing would necessitate appearing within the focus of Horner's gun. To hell with it! Beaupre scowled. If Irish escaped McCartrey's harvest there might still be some way...

Beaupre got up and strode irascibly about the room, fists jammed into his pockets. He did not throw away things for the fun of it, nor had he any intention of pitching this hand in if he could come across some means of putting the hex on that stinking McCartrey.

Teeth clamped savagely, he blew gray smoke like a fog about him as he tried to hit on some solution. He could bring in a U.S. marshal, sure; but that was no good if a man hoped for profit. The stakes were too high, the spoils too tempting, to throw the thing over just to hang onto life. He meant to play the hand out if he could stay on his feet. There must be some way of turning the tables, he thought, and went out to take a turn through the day's bright glare.

He walked around to collect the week's receipts from his restaurant, and the hasher said, 'You seen that medicine show?'

Beaupre, counting loose change, shook his head. The girl eyeing her reflection in the window, poked her hair. 'Somethin' about that feller ... I dunno what it is but I've sure seen that guy some place.'

Beaupre dropped the hard cash in his pockets and folded the currency up in a paper. He grinned at her, leaving. 'You've seen them all, Tillie.'

Outside, eyes narrowing against the sun's arc, he stared west and saw the outfit. Snake oil! The fellow didn't lack for an audience. Beaupre thought with contempt what fools people were. He stepped into the Palace, back again with McCartrey, without having cornered any likely solution.

Locking the receipts in the safe he sat down at his desk, and then, too much in ferment to be comfortable, jumped up and tramped over to stare bitterly through the grimy window.

There'd be pickings in this, fat pickings. McCartrey had his sights lined on Straddlebug, a vastly expanded Straddlebug that would include Fardel's lake and grass and the range pre-empted by the shoestring outfits scattered through those mountain meadows behind him.

Beaupre ground his teeth in an agony of envy, pitched away his mangled cigar and cursed irascibly. Why should McCartrey have all this? He knew enough of the fellow's plans to understand how Bates figured to swing it...

He sent a man looking for Clell, and, sloshing his hat on again, set off up the road to learn what sort of spiel was able to make gold out of snake oil.

Eight or ten people stood loosely grouped about the wagon, staring hypnotized at the bottle being held up for their inspection. Beaupre recognised them all—the blacksmith with rolled-up sleeves and bulging biceps, the baker in his apron teetering back on flour-spattered boot heels, the croupier from the Palace, the hasher from the Ophir, the near-sighted barber peering through his steel-rimmed cheaters, the night boss from the livery enrapturedly sucking on a barley stem... They looked, Beaupre thought uncharitably, not unlike those cud-chewing oxen and were displaying just about as much intelligence.

'... And remember, if you ain't convinced of improvement inside of six days you can have your money back—every dadburned penny! This oil is positively guaranteed to do every last thing I tell you it will, or you can call me a mule and I will waggle my ears. Now who wants a bottle? ... Here you are, ma'am, and thank you; it will put new sparkle in them teeth as sure as I'm standing here. If you get up in the morning with any sign of an ache—Thank you, sir, thank you ... This gentleman took home a bottle last night and here he is already back for another. Just look at that glow in his cheeks! I tell you, friends, if Ponce de Leon could have got his hands on a bottle of this stuff…'

Beaupre was watching the seller, not the bottle. The fellow stunk to high heaven. A grubby hawk-nosed man with a droopy mustache in a coonskin cap and dirty buckskin shirt that smelled of fire smoke and Indian. Wrinkling his nose in disgust Beaupre turned back towards town.

The man he had sent after Clell hadn't found him. Beaupre poured himself a drink and thought that, by God, there had to be some way to do this. Tonight, sure as hell, that bleached-eye Kid…

He wheeled away from the bar and went into his office, shoving the door shut with his heel. He shook the derringer out of his coat sleeve, replacing its load with fresh stock from his desk. About the only thing he could think of was to try to hire the Kid away from his present employment.

It was then that inspiration suddenly lit up his mind. Why not hire the Kid to put a slug through McCartrey?

*   *   *

A pallid sun was palely gilding the cobwebby windows when Irish reluctantly came out of his blankets, stomped feet into boots and reached around for his hat. This dry-country air could get colder than frog legs. He could see his breath as he struggled into his shirt.

152

With chattering teeth he got hold of his pants. A forty-degree change between midnight and noon took a deal of getting used to. Going around to the wash-bench he scowled at his reflection in the piece of cracked mirror.

He blamed the scanty lather when the razor nicked him twice. But one thing he had to hand cold water—it certainly woke a man up. Sharpened his appetite too. He ran a comb through his hair and went back inside, feeling strangely out of patience with this role he was playing. Cuffing dust off a sleeve he got into his coat, tied his tie and headed house-wards, made aware by the chimney he would find someone up.

He saw the Mexican forking hay to the penned stock. Several of the horses raised their heads to regard him warily. Primero went on with his work, paying no attention to him.

Irish, forgetting the man, had not taken three steps when he discovered where he'd gotten that impression of having seen Cherry before. She was the girl of the mirage—the buildings and their arrangement and the group of heads-down cattle stolidly browsing the fringe of the shore brought it back. The night had been too dark when he arrived for him to realize.

He stopped a moment, eyeing the lake, better able to understand now some of the feeling which had led Fick to consider taking over this outfit. That huge body of water with the fog rolling off it would have made all the difference to Fick in this emergency.

Irish was interested enough to walk around the nearer end of the lake, where, narrowing, it swung about the railed back porch to move eddying into a wire-meshed spillway provided to drop the overflow into the creek which normally watered the whole lower Basin. It was easy enough to see from this vantage that the creek had been here a long while before the dam which had backed up the water. There seemed hardly enough water falling over it now to make even mud more than half-way to town.

Irish, shaking his head, turned back. Small wonder Fick had gone on the warpath. With drought hanging over the country and cattle dying like flies no one outfit had any moral right to be sitting, like Crescent, on this much water.

Stepping onto the porch he was about to call out when he saw the man standing behind the door's tattered screen. It was hard through the bulgy mask of that rust to make out the man's features, but this, he guessed, must be Fardel. He smiled, 'I'm the preacher,' but the man didn't move.

There was an obstinate tenacity in the look of that anchored shape, an uncompromising truculence in the tone with which he said, 'If you've come out here to try and talk me into sharing that water you can get on your horse and start making tracks pronto!'

'It's the preacher, Pap,' Cherry called from the kitchen. 'Ask him in. We're about ready to set.'

Fardel stared a moment longer before he grudgingly stepped aside. 'You heard her. Come in if you don't mind taking the food right out of the mouths of my wife and daughter.'

He pushed open the screen and Irish stepped past him, so furious his mouth was a white-ridged line. He turned left in the entry and came into the kitchen's bright warmth and saw the women.

Cherry, bending over the stove with rolled sleeves, was in the tight dress again, her hair a golden halo seen this way against the sun. Her face, tipped forward, was half in shadow, but her smile was quick to reach for him as Fardel, letting the screen slam, added his presence to the gathering.

Irish looked at Fardel's wife and ducked his head as he put broad shoulders against a wall and stood there holding his hat like a fool. 'This is Chloe,' Fardel said, fixing a plate for her, and dropped into a chair at the head of the table without further remark.

Mrs Fardel looked vaguely at Irish and forgot him. Perhaps once she had been pretty, but all evidence of this was gone. She

155

was huge to the point of being grotesque, almost totally concealing the rugged chair she was ensconced in. Her out-thrust feet were bare and not particularly clean, and her near-white hair, cropped short like a squaw's, hung about her moonlike face in the tangled strings of a witch's bridle. Her arms were like hams and she began eating as soon as Fardel's butt touched the chair.

Cherry, faintly flushed, came up with the gravy and a plate of steaming corn bread. 'Set in, Parson,' she said, 'and start eating. We don't stand on ceremony here.'

It was in Irish's mind to say he wasn't hungry, but he was. And, since he would obviously be forced to impose on Crescent's hospitality for another several days unless he wished to be shot or taken, it was plain he must either starve for his scruples or look an even greater fool were he to let Fardel's words keep him away from the table now.

Swallowing his pride he drew up a chair and let the girl help him to fish and grits. She pressed the corn bread on him and told him to have some gravy. Then she came with the blessed aroma of coffee, and, when she had filled all the cups, sat down. 'Would you care to return thanks?' she said tightly.

Fardel, glaring, grudgingly lowered a laden fork, but his wife went right on with her chewing. Cherry bowed her blonde head and Irish, remembering his father,

156

murmured, 'God bless this food to our use and us to Thy service. In Christ's name we ask this. Amen.'

Fardel put the forkful of fish into his mouth and Cherry, stirring her coffee, said, 'Pap caught these before it got light. He thinks our lake has got the best fish in Arizona.'

'They're very good,' Irish said, and the old man snorted.

'Best fish you'll ever eat,' he said bluntly. 'I imported the stock from Pennsylvania Fisheries—it's not everyone could get them to live in this mud. Pickerel. Haven't any use for fish that won't fight. We've got black bass too, and muskies. I built this lake to fish in and I brought it back of the porch so my wife can fish too. Cost me half the cattle I started with to do it, so don't give me any palaver about sharing it.'

'This drought,' Irish said, 'has hit Straddlebug pretty bad.'

'And whose fault is that? *I* didn't overstock Fick's range.'

'You could help relieve his shortage of grass and water—'

'Look,' Fardel said, putting down his fork. 'When I came into this country there wasn't anyone around here but Indians, and that was the way I wanted it. We got along all right. I didn't bother them and they didn't bother me. When the country started settling up there was trouble with the Indians. The Government put in a couple of forts. That put the lid on the Indian troubles, but it laid no blight on the rustling and gunplay or the scramble for graze that came in with the syndicate. The fellow they had here in charge of it first got strung up one night by some of his neighbors, so that bunch in Chicago bought the most of them out.

'This gave them more room. East and south it fetched them up against me and gave me control of two-thirds of the creek, which was ample if they'd put in a man who understood cattle. Fick never has and never will.' He said, glaring at Irish as though he held him personally responsible, 'The man's a nincompoop and a blowhard, but I will give him credit for one thing. He had enough sense to hire a man who did know. That man, McCartrey, has made a good thing out of Straddlebug; he's a fireball, a pusher, a fellow that up till now has done every last thing Fick could have wanted.'

Fardel, observing the parson's increased interest, smiled thinly. 'Up till now, I said, Fick has had McCartrey with him. Beaupre, the big wheeze of Red Post, fetched a bunch of homesteaders into the Basin and Fick ran them out—at least he passed down the orders. But even a man of McCartrey's kidney has to draw the line somewhere. When Fick proposed to screw me out of this place McCartrey bowed up and quit.'

Boots scraped the boards of the porch. The screen door skreaked and the Mexican came in with a smile of apology, his dark eyes finding Cherry. At her nod he came round and, dropping his hat on the floor, pulled up a chair and sat down beside Irish. 'This is Antonio Primero,' Fardel said as the girl was filling up his plate. To the Mexican—'Our Red Post parson.'

Primero, pushing up, bobbed his head in a nod, face brightening when Irish put out a hand. He wiped his own on the leg of his pants before rather gingerly taking it. His lips came open in an expressionless grin. 'Honored,' he grunted, sinking back in his chair. He made the sign of the cross and with his elbows on the table fell to eating.

Irish's glance returned to Fardel. 'You say this range boss has quit Fick—you are sure?'

Cherry's amber eyes looked at Irish inscrutably. 'We have only his word for it. He came by last night and told us.'

'Out of his own mouth,' Fardel grinned. 'You couldn't get it any straighter.'

'He would have to go out of his way to come here.'

'He went out of his way. Fick is due for a jolt. McCartrey is throwing his weight in with us.' He reached, chuckling, over the table for his wife's empty plate and refilled it. Irish looked at Primero. The Mexican shrugged. Dropping back in his chair Fardel said to the girl, 'Your mother can use some more coffee.'

Cherry, still looking at Irish, went after it. Irish said, 'Talk is cheap.'

'We'll find out soon enough,' Fardel growled.

The girl came back with the chipped enamel pot. 'He said we must either fight or lose out here. I think it might be a good thing if we did.'

'Fighting's not the answer to anything.' Irish kept looking at Fardel until the old man glared back at him.

'All I want is to be let alone.'

'All you'll get from McCartrey is trouble. You think his kind would give you anything for nothing?'

'I know what he's after!'

'And are you willing for him to have it?'

'I'll take care of that when the time comes.'

Irish watched Primero wiping out his plate. 'He told Pap,' Cherry announced, 'we'd have to move those fellers before they got a shack up...'

'And when he understood we couldn't,' Fardel finished with sly malice, 'he said he would move them off himself. I guess that shows where he stands plain enough.'

It didn't actually show anything, but Irish let it ride. Pushing back he lifted a hand to

160

get a cigar from his pocket, and, remembering, carried the hand a little higher to rasp his chin. Habits were hard to get rid of and it was a habit of thought which was bolstering Fardel in the stand he was taking.

The man had been here so long he couldn't really envisage the possibility of a time when he would be here no longer. He was ignoring the vast difference between his own spread and Straddlebug, the disparity in size, the weight of men and guns that could be used, if they chose, to force their will upon him. He was an ostrich burying his head in the sand, leaning on McCartrey because Fick's ramrod had turned his coat, and believing because he wanted to that the man's lust would hold him loyal until the need of him was past.

Irish, admitting prejudice, had no faith in the man at all. McCartrey was a type he had met in a hundred places and the only thing you could bank on about him was that, in a pinch, he would look out for McCartrey.

He said, 'When a man's got his back to the wall it is conceivable he must fight, if for no other reason than to keep his self-respect. But your back, Mister Fardel, is not yet to the wall. You can ease the pressure. You've got a gate in that dam. You can put three feet of water—'

Fardel's fist slammed the table with such force the dishes jumped. 'I wouldn't give that stinker water if his tongue was hanging out a foot and forty inches!'

CHAPTER THIRTEEN

The brightening sun climbed higher into the breathless glare of the brassy sky. Day's heat closed over the Basin like a kind of blue smoke where the Roskruge Mountains, shimmering in the distance, lifted rock ribs above the dun monotony of the drought-stricken range. Nearer at hand the lush grass of Fardel's pastures appeared less succulent in the pitiless light, and the cattle, turning away from it, took shelter in what shade was afforded by the foot-hills to stand in bovine discomfort among thickets of scrub oak and cedar.

It was stifling in the bunkhouse even after Irish had forced open the windows, yet he grimly stayed, stretched out on a bunk with his shirt off, preferring this discomfort to the girl's brooding stare. He had no idea where the Mexican was off to, but the old man was out in a boat on the lake, and his gargantuan spouse drowsed in the meager shade of the railed back porch.

Irish found himself hard to understand this morning. His sole reason for coming here had been to keep under cover until the

162

sheriff became disgruntled enough to call off his hunt. What happened to Fardel was no concern of his, yet he kept thinking of the man, still stewing over Crescent's problems. Preposterous? He was doing it. And it wasn't because of Fardel's daughter, though she also was taking up thought that should more reasonably have been devoted to his own situation, which, while not yet strictly urgent, might easily become disastrous.

There was Beaupre, for example, with his threat of going to Haines; and McCartrey, who had put Clell onto him. And that bleach-eyed Kid who would certainly never rest until his hatred was dissolved in gun smoke.

Irish strove to put the Fardels out of his mind, becoming in his failure increasingly irascible, until at last, swearing bitterly, he got up and flung into his shirt and shoulder harness.

He took out his gun and cleaned it and put the cartridges back in its chambers with his angry thoughts still circling between the girl and her father's problems. He was not immune to the desires of the flesh and was completely aware of how far Cherry would go to get away from this environment. A phrase out of Scripture passed through his mind and he sheathed the big pistol and caught up his coat, thinking to tramp through the woods until his thoughts were collected. But as he reached for his hat he heard steps at the door and, looking up, saw Cherry standing there.

He saw reproach in her eyes. She came into the room, not speaking but considering him in the half-bold, watchful way she had with all of her attention. She came quite near and stood a moment, allowing him to sense the feel of her presence.

He heard in this brittle stillness the shifting of Fardel's body in the boat out on the lake. Sweat burst through the pores of his skin, and the brim of his hat, where he clutched it, crumpled. He said through stiff lips, 'I was going for a walk,' and a kind of wonder touched her face and she took hold of his arm, faintly trembling.

'Take me with you.'

She felt the unyielding stiffness of him and tipped back her head to search his expression with eyes that became inexpressibly wistful. 'Was it so bad of me to come here?'

Somehow he had known she would come; it was this knowledge all his thinking had been trying to cover up. Aroused and angrily at odds with himself he said, 'I don't know,' and backed away from this thing that was building between them.

He put on his hat with its sedate parson's flatness, glancing towards the door; but she would not leave this so. She ran her hand up his arm, clutching it fiercely, shaking him.

'Please.'

He took Cherry's arm and saw how enormously she was lifted. His voice was gruff. 'Do you know a path?'

'Oh, I do! Through the woods...'

He followed her out and around the corrals with the sun's blinding light beating up from the earth, and across bare ledges of shelf rock where wind had torn the loose soil away. He looked over his shoulder when they were half-way to the trees and saw the lake far below and, in the middle distance, the roofs of Red Post's buildings.

It brought things back and he shook his head, unconsciously frowning as he climbed the meandering trail in her wake, and so came into the trees where she waited. She smiled, taking his arm, 'Ain't that coat pretty hot?'

'I can stand it.'

There was wind up here. He watched it ruffle her hair. 'You're out of breath,' she smiled. 'We'd better rest.'

Turning loose from his arm she dropped onto the brown matting of needles. She put her back to a rock and hugged her knees and he was glad enough to drop beside her. The unaccustomed exertion on top of the heat and this coat made the shirt feel like a wet rag where it touched him. He stretched out on an elbow with the cool slickness under him, watching the play of light and shadow

165

across her face.

She stared off into the blue. 'I used to come here a lot when I was younger. Sometimes I would be Cortez or Pizarro; once I was Father Kino... Do you think he would have minded?'

The picture her words called up hit him hard and he bent his head, scowling at the earth his fingers had cleared of the pines' shed foliage. He traced a series of half-formed patterns, irritably clearing the ground of each one before replacing it with another even more ill-favored doodle. He said at last to break the stillness, 'Why'd you quit? I mean, coming up here.'

Her shoulders lifted into a shrug. 'Outgrew it, I guess. I found this other place. You can't see so much there.'

His glance tipped up, discovering her soberness. He said from sudden conviction, 'I don't believe you know what you do to a man,' and saw the brightness of her smile chase all the soberness away. It bothered him to learn she could be pleased with so very little.

His eyes, as she got up, observed the grace of her rising figure and his mouth pinched into a dissatisfied line. She reached down a hand and he rose with an increasing reluctance. She smiled, twisting round to look back at him. Then she was into the brush and Irish followed, softly cursing.

166

Trees closed them in, shutting out with dark tops the blue gleam of the sky; and this melancholy gloom, so cathedral-like, became distantly alive with the cry of the wind. Narrow shafts of sunlight, striking through the churn of that lofty foliage, picked out bright splotches of strawberry bark; and the smell of pitch was strong in these woods.

He was aware of the litheness ahead of him, of the sway of her skirt. Cramps ached through his muscles.

Fleeting thoughts of Pauline came unbidden, and the nails of clenched fingers cut the sweat on his palms, but he did not turn back. And when the girl swung to face him he sucked in his breath.

He felt her tremble as their mouths met, and there was nothing in this moment but the two of them locked together. Then she twisted away with a shaken laugh and stepped back, deeply breathing.

She sprang away, almost running, but slowed where the lift of a knob rose more steeply. There she turned, excitedly smiling; and he plunged after her, angry, impatient, with his greater stride gaining so rapidly that when she stopped abruptly he almost ran into her. His glance, going across the rigidity of her shoulder, discovered Primero.

The Mexican, completely still, was sitting a freckled grey gelding at the farther rim of this saucerlike depression with the pines at his back and his ungloved hands in front of him. A pale wisp of smoke ribboned away past his cheek from the hand-rolled cigarette in the corner of his mouth, and his eyes, slightly narrowed, stared back at them unwinking.

'I guess,' Irish said, 'this is about as far as we'd better go before lunch.'

CHAPTER FOURTEEN

But he wasn't fooled and Primero was not either.

Pitching away his smoke the Mexican got down, politely offering the girl his mount. Irish saw her eyes as she whirled, moving off across the slope like a tawny cat. His glance touched Primero, and, seeing how precariously the man was balanced, he left the silence alone. Turning leisurely he followed the swishing flounce of Cherry's skirt.

There was a man's natural regret in Irish now but no real anger. He felt compassion for them both and this was not unmixed with worry, but mostly what he felt was a sense of release, of burdens lifted. This was conscience, that inexplicable inner compulsion whose clamor had so often amused him.

168

He heard Primero, behind him, get into his saddle, and the measured clop-clop of the grey gelding's hoofs. This dimmed out on the needles but again shortly lifted as they crossed harder ground.

Pauline's face came before him clearly, almost as if she were trying to tell him something, and then dissolved in the report of a shod hoof striking rock.

He didn't like the sound of Primero back there. The idea of the man so deliberately pacing along in their wake was repugnant to Irish and just a little unnerving. This thought brought the Kid back into his head and he knew he wasn't done with that either. He remembered Clell and with a tightening of muscles something else clicked into place. *If McCartrey had hired Clell how had Beaupre been able to call Clell off?*

It was in a very thoughtful frame of mind that Irish once again came to Fardel's headquarters. He walked around the corrals in the blazing noon light with the heat of the sun coming up through his boots, and had a careful look at his rented dun. The horse was rough but well put together, with a free-swinging stride and plenty of muscling inside and out. It was built for endurance and, with that long underline, had a fair burst of speed which Irish had already tested. But neither of these things would get him past Haines' hunting posses. From the heights, coming down, he had seen activity in the north of the Basin and that same patrol would be extended through the mountains. The sheriff's noose of steel was closing. Any move towards flight would be fatal.

He bent his steps towards the bunkhouse, and at the door saw Fardel getting out of his boat. Three gleaming fish with a rope through their gills threw out splinters of light as the old man headed for the house.

Irish went in and sat down on his bunk; then got up to stand by the single front window, watching Primero taking care of his horse. Even after the man went to wash his hands at the bench Irish stood there, bleakly staring. But he followed the Mexican over to the house when Fardel stuck his head out to yell, 'Come and get it.'

There was a lean near-hidden strength in the whipcord lines of Primero's high-heeled body. His every movement was gracefully supple and there was intelligence at work in his head. The man was no ordinary chili-eating drifter. A good talk between them might clear up some wrong ideas; but, even as he thought this, Irish knew they would never have it. Some things you couldn't talk about and one of these was a woman.

Fish and grits and baking soda biscuits. It was a pretty glum meal. Fardel's wife, busily stuffing, never contributed a word and the several attempts Irish made to be sociable petered out in the brevity of the indifferent response. The girl didn't lift her eyes from her plate. Primero sat stiffly with his sultry thoughts and only poked at his food. Twice Irish caught him staring fixedly at the girl, and once, looking up, found himself to be the recipient of that smouldering regard. When he was finished Primero, excusing himself, departed.

Against his better judgment Irish said to Fardel finally, 'I can't help thinking that fellow, McCartrey, is out to do you.'

Fardel refilled his wife's plate and said mildly, 'Time will tell.'

Irish considered the rancher with a shortening temper. He was not a particularly large man, although, hunched forward as he was, you might get that impression. His sandy hair was becoming thin on top and the down-curling ends of his ragged mustache showed the stain of a confirmed and careless user of snuff. He looked, Irish thought, about the way Beaupre had described him, a kind of cross between impoverished gentility and the bluster of a share-cropper. 'But will it tell soon enough for you to save this place if he's after it?'

'Better him, if he is, than that two-by-four Fick.'

'What about your wife and daughter?'

Fardel put the flats of both hands on the table. He'd been drinking again and it showed in his eyes. 'I'll take care of my family—'

'At least,' Irish said, 'we could go out there and see if he has moved those fellows off.'

Fardel's stare turned bright with truculence. It was plain he resented the supposed parson's interference, but he did not react as Irish had looked for him to. Some restraint from his past locked the anger in his throat. 'Very well,' he said gruffly, 'we'll just do that. Get your horse.'

*   *   *

Primero, dourly perched atop the corral, watched Irish saddle. This surveillance was annoying. Irish thought as he jerked the latigo tight it was getting so that practically everything annoyed him. He was filled with internal commotion, and no wonder. He had enough on his mind without worrying about Fardel, but it went against the grain to see the man made such a fool of.

Fardel's stubborn hatred of Fick was laying him wide open to whatever McCartrey was up to. Fardel couldn't stand against Fick, no matter what he thought, and it was beginning to look, in Irish's opinion, as though McCartrey was the nigger in both the Fick and Fardel woodpiles.

It was Clell, of course, who had inspired this suspicion. Clell hired by McCartrey and called off by Anton Beaupre. Clell, in Irish's mind, had tied the pair of them together. And now this McCartrey was hatching out a deal with Crescent.

It was not unnatural, all things considered, that Irish should be finding himself more than a little distracted. But his irritability—the rock bottom and inescapable basis of this turmoil—sprang not so much from outside sources as from the unresolved conflict of contradictory facets of his own ungovernable personality. Quirks, if you will—like this fright that lay in wait for him at the thought of physical violence.

Too well he understood his faults, but not well enough to master them. His dislike of being unkind, for example, had backed him into more than one scrape and might as easily have gotten him killed if he hadn't all his life been keeping his guard up against it. He disliked involvement and diligently sought to avoid responsibility, which he considered the end result of gathering moss and more substantial possessions, and was why he hadn't accumulated any. Yet in spite of this belief, despite his lifelong fight against it, he had ironically within his nature a vast sense of responsibility.

This was the cross he'd carried through thirty-two years of living—kindness constantly quarrelling with his ingrown desire to be let alone; his sense of responsibility versus dread of having to assume it.

Stealing a covert glance at Primero he shoved the tongue of the buckle into the strap, and straightened. He felt sorry for Fardel, but the rancher's blindness was in no sense a burden to be put on him, nor had he any intention of attempting to lift it. He was going to that camp for his own information, not for any aid this might give the girl's father. He felt sorry for the girl too, but not as sorry as he had.

Turning now he met Primero's regard. 'The *patron* is riding with me for a look at what McCartrey has accomplished. If you will tell me which horse he favors...'

'I thought mebbe you were going from here away. For good,' the Mexican added. Then Fardel came from the house and Primero, quitting his place, went into the larger corral with his rope and snagged a big bay with a snip on its nose which he readied and led out without further remark.

Fardel thrust a Sharp's rifle into the case under the fender and, still riled, climbed into the saddle. He sent the bay south-east along the line of the creek, Irish silently following. The Mexican's stare made his back muscles prickle, and in this fashion, single file, they rode perhaps a quarter-mile before the old

174

man, drawing rein, asked, 'How long you figuring to be with us?'

'Expect I'll stick around until you're done with this business.'

Fardel, glowering, went on. Some twenty minutes later, yanking the Sharp's, he fired at a coyote, swearing when the animal disappeared among the thickets flanking the willows along the creek.

This range, Irish noticed, was still in pretty fair shape. It was rolling ground mostly, with very little brush. Fick's homesteaders were probably gone, he reflected; for whatever McCartrey had up his sleeve he'd want first to convince Fardel of his good faith, and he could hardly do this without moving them off. So Irish wasn't surprised when, about two miles from their start, Fardel, pointing, drew up. 'Yonder's their camp. And no horses. No damn building either!'

Irish kept riding.

'Where you going?'

'Figuring to have that look.'

'Hell,' Fardel said, kneeing his bay up alongside, 'there's no point in going closer. If they were there we'd see their horses.'

Irish, not bothering to answer, kept edging the dun watchfully forward, eyes quartering the trampled tangle of graze and wishing he had spent more time reading sign. It looked as though Fardel had the right of it, but having come this far Irish meant to make sure.

Back at headquarters the grass stood hip high, but here, where the creek was reduced to a trickle, it reached up only to the dun's knobby knees. Plenty deep enough, though, to hide a man with a rifle—or a dozen, he thought grimly.

He saw the litter of scattered foodstuffs, a side of pork, a burst sack of beans, a coffee pot battered and twisted beyond use. He stood up in his stirrups for a better look, not liking this.

Trouble smell hung in the air like burnt cordite.

Fardel came up and stopped beside him, also staring. But whereas Irish showed only the wooden face of a gambler, the rancher made no effort to hide his feelings. 'Run them off and wrecked their camp,' he said with an evident satisfaction.

'That mean—' Irish grumbled, and abruptly stiffened. Beyond the dirt-smeared greasy shine of it he saw, thrust out of the grass at an impossible angle, the lower half of a boot with the sun winking off its bent-over spur.

The hairs along the back of Irish's neck began to crackle. Fardel—seeing it now—galvanized into sudden movement, dragged the heavy Sharp's from beneath his knee and sent his horse plunging forward.

Irish had no opportunity to discover what

he was up to. Before the old man was half across the sunstruck distance a second rider, much nearer, broke from the creekside willows and, coming up out of leather, clapped rifle to shoulder and played an *obbligato* that cut the quiet to pieces.

Fardel never had a chance. The first shot tore through his hat. The second got him.

Even as the old man's arms flailed out, flung unbalanced against the cantle by the shock of the bullet's impact, Irish was quitting the dun. He saw the ground coming up—struck hard and rolled desperately, hearing the continuing slam of that rifle through the scream of his horse and the spat-spat around him.

The man was firing too fast. He had the magazine emptied before Irish was able to get hold of his pistol. As Bert came on to a knee in the chattering echoes he saw the man, swung around, tearing off through the creek brush.

Filled with rage though he was Irish lowered the pistol. He knew with the seething fury of frustration the range was too great, and watched the Kid disappear.

When the hoof sound was gone he went over to Fardel. There wasn't anything he could do for him. Tramping back to the dun he found a like situation. He caught the old gent's bay, picked up the Sharp's, and had a go-round with the animal before he could get

177

Fardel's body across the saddle.

He used Fardel's rope. Then he went over and had his grim-eyed look at the fellow whose boot they had seen before the advent of Horner. He had an ineffectual face and had been shot through the back at close range, probably pistolled. There was no doubt at all in Irish's mind that this was one of Fick's homesteaders.

He considered the sun. He spread his coat over the rancher and, leading the bay, struck out for headquarters.

CHAPTER FIFTEEN

Two and a half miles was a lot easier thought about than walked, Irish discovered—particularly with boots on. But it afforded plenty of time for speculation and conjecture.

Night lay over the yard when he came into the lamp-laced shadows, wearily plodding ahead of the bay's silent burden. Primero materialized out of the gloom, staring hard at the coat-shrouded shape as Irish talked but saying nothing until the girl, brought off the veranda by Irish's voice, came up to them in the shaft of light the left-open door flung after her.

'It's your dad,' Irish said, and tersely told

178

of Fardel's shooting.

He could not make out her expression with the light spearing into his face the way it was, but he was prepared for the calm acceptance in which she asked if he were sure the man was Horner, and for the Mexican's evident suspicion when he said, 'Yes.' He had known when they'd come upon the man this morning he would be hearing further from Primero. The very fact of his being up there...

He said, 'It's now obvious McCartrey intended from the start to flimflam your father. For reasons of his own I think he wants a range war and has taken the shortest cut.'

It was plain from the way his lips curled what the Mexican thought, but Irish ignored him. 'There's little doubt that fellow we found with the hole through his back was one of the pair Fick put to squatting on this place. Nothing else makes sense. The other, whoever he was, apparently was gone when McCartrey showed up. By shooting that fellow he has made it appear that your dad came over there with blood in his eye—that, in short, Crescent's owner has resorted to gunplay. And by the manner of this killing he has given the Basin little cause to love Crescent or be unduly concerned about what happened to your father.'

'You are trying to tell me,' Cherry said,

179

completely sober, 'that I can look for no help from Red Post—is that it?'

Irish nodded. 'He cut you off from help when he drygulched that fellow. Some will think the man got what he was asking for, but, anticipating Straddlebug's wrath and remembering Straddlebug's size, the other outfits around here will call it a private feud and keep out of it.'

She came up nearer, put a hand on his arm. He could not see her eyes but he could feel them searching his face. 'We could sell out?'

Irish shrugged. 'To McCartrey, possibly. I doubt it—'

'You do not need to sell out!' Primero broke in fiercely. 'Below the border I have friends. Many mens who will come—'

'Tony, be still,' Cherry said without moving her eyes. 'You don't think he would give me a fair price for it?'

'You know the man better than I do.'

She let go of his arm, remaining silent so long Irish thought she was angry. She may have been. It didn't show when she said, with her voice softly begging. 'If I hold on you'll see me through?'

'What can this one do? A priest!' Primero exploded. 'Guns are all that will stop those peegs! *Chingado!*' he growled, seizing onto her arm, spinning her round in his fury. 'Do not be afraid! I will take care of these *gringos*

180

for you!'

She jerked loose of his grip, imploring eyes seeking Irish.

Irish was studying the Mexican thoughtfully. 'How many men can you find?'

Primero spat contemptuously. 'I was not talking to you!'

'Would you talk to hard cash?'

The Mexican glared, saying nothing.

Cherry moved nearer Irish, half turning in the lamplight so that now it struck across her, boldly moulding her curves to new meaning.

But Irish's thoughts were not on her. He was seeing her father spilling out of that saddle, glimpsing the larger picture of what his slaying and the brutal murder of that squatter spelled for this Basin if McCartrey were not stopped. He had been intending all along, of course, to stay; so he said now, 'I'll do what I can.'

He could tell by the way she watched him this was not the answer she wanted, but after a moment she smiled, and this made him vaguely uneasy, so that he said to change the subject, 'I'd better be taking your father to town...'

'Primero will do that. I want—'

'This whole business will have to be reported to the sheriff.'

She said impatiently, 'Tony can take care of that.'

'*Seguro*—of a certainty. A loyal man, thees Tony.' Primero said with a tight hard smile. 'He will tell them in town the truth; how thees priest have persuade your father to go with him to thees camp where he could kill him and that other one.'

Irish heard the sharp gasp of the girl's indrawn breath, felt her hand clutch his sleeve. 'That's all right,' he said quietly. 'While you're at it you can tell them how I did this without a rifle. Tell them anything you want, then get those friends of yours and come back here.'

The girl caught his arm. 'You're going to fight?'

'Not that way. Only the little ones have to use force. When you're big enough people steer clear of you. If Primero will fetch his friends there won't be any fight—if he gets back here in time. I'll take your dad into town while Primero rides after them.' He looked at the Mexican. 'That suit you?'

Primero's eyes, in the light, were black glass. He took his time about answering, his distrustful stare narrowly raking Irish's face as though he would uncover some *Yanqui* trick in this, finally ducking his head in a grudging nod. 'But only,' he told Cherry, 'if he goes. You understand?'

Color darkened her cheeks. 'Are you afraid to have him stay?'

'Is an eagle afraid—' The man broke it off,

his chin-strapped face canted to the left as though listening. Irish heard nothing, but the Mexican, suddenly straightening, stepped out of the light. Irish, wheeling, caught it then, faint at first but increasingly plainer. The up-and-down cadence of a fast-running horse.

Emulating the Mexican he blurred into the shadows, remembering Haines and the closing noose of that manhunt, not supposing a connection but prepared to take no chances in view of Beaupre's threat. Now as the sound swept nearer he became aware of its rhythm, his subconscious translating this into knowledge.

The horse was faltering; was therefore either wounded or had carried its rider beyond common call.

He took his hand off the gun, slipping quietly forward as the horse rounded the house and came with its awful breathing up through the darkness at a lurching stagger.

'*Quien es?*' the Mexican called, his voice spider-thin with the constriction of tension. Irish, still moving, heard the click of a gunlock. 'Never mind,' he said grimly. 'Keep back and I'll get him.'

Gathering himself, he clenched his jaw and bitterly waited. But as horse and rider loomed before him, a more solid black against the blackness around them, he straightened out of his crouch, realizing an enemy would not come in this fashion.

'Pull up,' he said quietly. 'You're with friends. What's all the rush for?'

He caught a startled gasp, saw the flutter of elbows. The horse came to a stop. It had no collection; stood wobbling, head hanging between its shading, tottery legs.

The rider swayed, and as he caught her Irish knew with a terrible despair splintering through him that the girl in his trembling arms was Pauline.

CHAPTER SIXTEEN

McCartrey, damning his luck after losing the girl, yanked his horse about viciously and sent it pelting towards Straddlebug. But gradually as he rode the angry resentment and frustration became replaced with cooler thinking and he permitted the horse to drop into a walk.

Let her go to Fardel's. This was one more nail he could drive into Fick's coffin. By God, he'd pay her back and more! Before he got through with this stinking Basin...

Lost in the comforting visions evoked by the confidence which his scheming inspired. McCartrey lallygagged along until he had each facet of this deal in perfect sequence. Then he kicked the horse into action, driving it through the silent dark at a headlong run towards the distant wink of Straddlebug's lights.

Drumming its ribs with the gouge of his spurs he built up this speed with no care for the horse beyond convincing himself it would last till they got there. Bates McCartrey had an impression to make and if he had to kill the nag making it that was all right with him.

Floundering up the last rise he added the quirt to the agony of sharp Spanish rowels. The horse went down in the yard and McCartrey never looked back at it. Fick stood on the porch beside a man with a lantern, and even before he reached them Bates could see that Fick was scared.

'Hell's to pay!' he shouted; and then, blackly scowling as he tramped up, 'Where's the rest of this bunch? What's the matter with the lamps?'

'I—I put them out when I heard your racket.' Fick considered him nervously, backing off a little from him. 'Where's Pauline? Did she—'

'I'll git to that. Where's the rest of the hands? Git 'em up! What I got to say,' McCartrey grumbled, 'concerns the whole outfit.'

Fick's eyes dived around like bot-flies. He licked at his lips and mustered a semblance of defiance that by the smell on his breath he had been priming for all evening. But his voice bled all the sap from it, adolescently cracking as he blurted in a rush to get it said before his wind quit: 'They're out pushing our stuff back into the hills.'

McCartrey stared a bleak moment and suddenly flung out his hands. 'I'm through! I won't work for a man who's got no more pride than you got.'

'You can't quit me now!' Fick cried, his voice jumping into high C.

'I've already done it.' McCartrey showed his contempt. 'I warned you, by God. Time after time. But you was bound to freeze folks out an' grab their range an' now you've had it. You fetched your ambition to the well once too frequent when you had us stake out Crescent to cut that old man off from his water.'

Fick's eyes were like holes burned in a bedsheet. 'I—I don't know what you're talking about...'

'Then you better be findin' out damn quick. That dive-keeper's just about fit to call the law in! Walker's dead an' the Kid's disappeared! Fardel's grabbed Pauline—'

With a strangled cry, both hands jerking heart-ward, Fick swayed and, collapsing, struck the planks of the porch all spraddled out. McCartrey, irascibly swearing as he bent over him, got hold of a wrist and growled, 'Fetch me some water!' to the man standing back of him.

The fellow set down his lantern, took a couple of uncertain steps and, wheeling, said, 'I dunno where any water is.'

McCartrey's head came round and he spun out of his crouch to come up with eyes blazing, face livid with anger. 'Clell! What're you doing here?'

'I come out to find out was there anythin'—'

'Didn't I tell you—'

'Now wait a minute,' Clell scowled. 'I ain't give nothin' away. I only been here a hour or so an' all I said was—'

'Never mind,' McCartrey's face was dark now. 'Go catch up your bronc an' get a saddle on that bald-faced chestnut in the far pen. We're gettin' out of here.'

'He gonna croak?' Clell said, staring down at Fick curiously.

'Him?' McCartrey snorted. 'No such luck! Now look, here's what you do—'

'What're you goin' to be doin'?'

McCartrey's eyes darkly glittered. Like most who are inclined to take themselves a little too seriously Bates McCartrey was easily angered and at any other time would have shown his bitter intolerance of both Clell's tone and question. But he had too much at stake to risk estranging the man at this juncture.

'I've got to locate my stock and find

187

somebody to move it,' he said, biting down on his temper. 'It's lucky for me you happened to drift out here. You go on into town and start the word around about Crescent jumping that homesteader camp. Play up Walker's killin'—shot in the back was the way I got it. Say the Kid's disappeared. Tell 'em Fardel's grabbed ... No, don't mention the girl; tell 'em Fick's about ready to burst his surcingle—which he will be when he comes outa that. He'll be on the peck sure.' He slapped Clell on the back. 'If this is handled right you can make a good thing of it. Never mind that chestnut, you git right on to town.'

Clell said, 'Is that guy Walker sure-enough kilt?'

'He won't never be no deader. Go an' look for yourself if you—'

'An' you're washed up here? You're sure-enough walkin' out on this outfit?'

'I've stuck with that bastard too long already. I tried to steer the damn fool away from this Fardel deal, but he's plumb bound an' determined to have that water! I quit him day before yesterday; he wouldn't pay me off but I'm collectin' right now,' McCartrey said, throwing a scowl at Fick.

'He didn't sound to me like he was fixin' to crowd Fardel.'

McCartrey said, laughing it off. 'You don't know that old bugger like I do. He's a great one for talkin' but all his talk's for the record; it don't gee with his orders. Chousin' his cows back into the hills! He's havin' them rounded up now to throw 'em onto Fardel's grass. Fardel ain't blind—that's why he jumped them two fellers.' He gave Clell a look. 'Hell! You don't think Beaupre's squatters was shoved outa this Basin without Fick passed down the orders?'

'But I thought you an' Beaupre—'

'Sure. I seen he made a fool of you. That's how come I never jumped you about turnin' that damn snooper loose. You let me do the thinkin', Clell, and we'll both of us be a heap better off.'

He went over and picked up the lantern, considered the syndicate manager a moment, then strode off towards the bunkhouse to pick up his belongings, hoping Clell would take the hint and get going. The man was beginning to wear a bit on him and, while he didn't have brains enough to be dangerous, it might be smart to arrange...

When he stepped out of the bunkhouse with his war sack Clell was gone. McCartrey got a rope and went into the corral. He dropped a noose on the bald-faced chestnut and got the animal ready for travel, reassembling certain facets of his plan while he was doing so. 'That goddam Clell,' he said abruptly, and rode across the yard to look at Fick again.

The resident manager was still unconscious.

Getting down, McCartrey went into the house. There was a safe in Fick's office. He didn't need any light to open it. He found the payroll and a couple of hundred extra, and shoving these bills in his pockets shut the safe and twirled the dial. Getting onto his feet he went back to the porch. Fick was still out.

McCartrey grinned a little then and, picking up the lantern, got aboard the waiting horse. Wheeling the animal away a few steps he swung the lantern, watching it break against the house, his grin broadening as burning oil spread over the porch's heavy planking and orange tendrils of flame leapt up the drenched siding of the tinder-dry wall.

'So long, sucker!' With a deep-throated chuckle he sent the horse towards town.

*   *   *

He had one briefly bad moment when his eyes, pulling off to the side, encountered the horse he'd ridden in on, observing the gear still on it. With a snort he said to hell with it. There wasn't nobody going to be asking him questions.

He had at first been inclined to ride into the hills and hunt up the crew, saying Fick wanted the stock put on Crescent. But why risk further involvement? He had things going the way he wanted them now. Putting paint on the lily was the way these amateurs stepped into rope. Smart thing to do was make sure of Beaupre and get rid of Clell. And just as quick as he got a good feed inside him this was what McCartrey aimed to take care of.

CHAPTER SEVENTEEN

Irish, more disturbed than he had been since coming here, silently carried the girl in the direction of the veranda, where Cherry stood with a rifle beside the open door. He heard the Mexican behind him and saw the expression on Cherry's face as he came into the light. She did not speak but there was no mistaking the trend of her thoughts. Her eyes were coldly hostile.

Pauline's hand pushed against Irish's chest. 'Put me down. I can stand.'

Across her shoulder and coppery hair Irish's glance locked with Cherry's, finding no give in it, nothing but outrage and anger. 'This girl needs rest,' he said brusquely, and shoved past her into the house.

He hooked a black rocker around with his foot, hearing the clank of Primero behind

191

him and, as he lowered the girl into it, the savage strike of Cherry's heels. 'Take your time,' he said quietly. 'You've got the whole night to talk.' His glance swung to Cherry. 'We could do with some coffee.'

She pulled breath harshly into her lungs and it seemed for a moment as though she meant to defy him. There were green flecks, hard as jade, in the metallic amber of her stare, and her cheeks looked taut as stretched drum-hide. Then she whirled and was gone, flinging out of the room like an angry cat.

Irish saw the strained shape of Primero's dark face, the white knuckles of the fists that were clenched at his sides.

He turned back to Pauline, observing her bewilderment. 'We're a little shook up ourselves,' he said wryly. 'I've just come in with her father from—'

'Where is Mr Fardel?'

Primero spoke before Irish could find a suitable reply. 'Dead!' he cried bitterly. 'Murdered—*es verdad*—by one of those dogs your father put on our grass!'

Irish told the story of their trip to the homesteaders' camp.

Pauline's face registered shock and anguish. Incredulity and bafflement were in the wide dark stare that searched his look and the Mexican's. 'But my father would never—' She broke off as at some sudden thought, and Primero said, 'Thees man is dead. Shot with rifle.'

'There's some mistake,' Pauline said. 'Dad—'

'You deny he put those mans on thees grass?'

'McCartrey might have done it,' Irish said, 'without Fick's knowledge.'

The Mexican's look was not perhaps as sceptical as Primero would have had it, but Irish's attention was all on the girl. Her odd-set eyes seemed queerly troubled and she said on an in-dragged breath, 'I don't know. There's something... Maybe "tension" isn't the word, but you can feel—it's like a cold wind blowing down the back of your neck. Dad's aged. There's ... Sometimes you'd almost think he was afraid of Bates McCartrey.'

Her eyes looked darker as they stared up at him. She was a maturer person than she had seemed on the stage. As though something, he thought, had suddenly caused her to grow up. And she was, he now realized, really beautiful. She was not relaxed, was very plainly on edge, but she was completely in command of both her mind and her emotions. Now, with hands locked together in her lap, she explained how she came to be here, how McCartrey had tried to run her down. 'I'm afraid I lost all sense of direction,' she said, smiling wryly but with no sign of embarrassment. 'All I could think of was getting away from him.'

'Have you any idea where you lost him?'
She shook her head. 'Not even when.' She stood up. 'If I can borrow a horse...'

'You can't go home tonight,' Irish said, and stood thoughtfully frowning. Cherry came in with the pot and four cups, which she handed around without opening her mouth. Irish saw Primero watching her. She contained her anger with better grace, even giving the Mexican a tight-lipped smile. 'No,' she said, looking coolly at Irish, 'you had better stay here. Parson will take you home tomorrow.'

Irish finished his coffee and set down the cup. When the others were emptied she gathered them up, going off to the kitchen, Primero following her.

Irish was glad of the chance to have Pauline alone. But before he could frame what he wanted to say to her Fardel's horse nickered and one farther off answered. The girl's eyes locked with Irish's while they listened to the unhurried cadence of an approaching rider.

A man's voice lifted just beyond the veranda as the hoof sound ceased. Irish, turning away, crossed the room and opened the door.

'Evening, Parson. Name's Beaupre, in case you've forgotten.' Saddle leather skreaked as the man swung down uninvited.

He came into the light and said, faintly smiling, 'You don't seem overjoyed to see me. If you'll move back from that door I'll come in and set awhile.'

*   *   *

When McCartrey reached town the hour was late but there was still some racked horses standing hip-shot at the Palace tie-rail. He rode near enough to see that one of them was Clell's, but he could not locate Horner's and drew back into the shadows irritably wondering where the man was.

Not that it made any great amount of difference. The only question in Bates' mind was whether the Kid had fixed that preacher. He circled round to the rear of the place and, there dismounting, approached a window, being careful to move where the gloom afforded most cover.

He saw Clell at the bar with a knot of men around him. The most of these were townsmen. Kreimer, of the Flying X, was there and a couple of the Boxed O punchers, and Clell was in fine fettle. You could tell by dropped jaws and bugged eyes the fellow was really doing a job on them.

McCartrey, chuckling, stepped nearer, curious to learn how Beaupre was taking it. But he couldn't see the dive-keeper; and Kreimer's voice, raised in sudden fury, leapt

195

through the closed window. 'By grab, if he's that kind of snake we better stomp him right now!'

A tightness came over Bates McCartrey's face. Oddly puzzled and strangely uneasy, he turned away from the window; then, stepping catfootedly closer, pressed an ear to the wall and stood rigidly listening, every muscle and sinew of his body drawn tight as he heard Clell say, 'All's I know is what I seen, an' I sure as hell seen him bash that lantern ag'in the front of the house.'

'And Fick,' Kreimer said, 'was still layin' on the porch?'

'You're goddam right!'

'The place was burnin' when he left?'

McCartrey's teeth rebelled in anguish from the pressure of grinding jaws as he stepped back from the wall in a berserk rage and lifted the gun from his holster. It was still only Clell's word against his own, but all he could think of was to shut the man's mouth. Kreimer, moving just as McCartrey fired, stumbled forward, pitching into the bar, and went down. McCartrey, cursing, emptied his pistol, shooting as fast as he could trigger, and with the last shot saw Clell buckle.

He walked back to his horse and climbed into the saddle. Still swearing under his breath he reloaded his piece and, bitterly scowling, shoved it into creaking leather. He sat there awhile with his hand on it then, listening to the hubbub breaking out through the town, to the shouting and calling and the sound of running feet. No chance now to learn about Beaupre or that snoop they'd sent in here making out to be a parson and whom he'd set down as a gambler that night he'd first seen him. No time to be hunting that damned Kid either.

Then his mind took up slack and, suddenly grinning, he eased the chestnut around, and walked him softly north away from the buildings, there turning him east at a quicker gait until he was east of the town a good quarter of a mile. Again turning the horse he drove it with his spurs into a dead run down the street, hauling it back on its haunches in a skittering stop squarely in front of Beaupre's Palace.

He swung down. Leaving the horse on dropped reins he strode through the dust and ducked under the hitch-rail, pushing men off his elbows as he stepped onto the porch. He shoved through the batwings and stopped with his burly shape just inside, ignoring the twisting heads and gaping mouths, centering his bleak glance on the havoc he'd created.

Kreimer, he saw, was stretched flat on the floor, Clell beside him, both of them obviously, indubitably dead. 'That goddam Kid!' he said, and, staring past the bandaged shoulder of one of the Boxed O punchers, focussed his bitter gaze on the fellow who was being held down while Haskins probed.

The man's groans didn't bother him any more than the white-faced stares this crowd turned on him. He revelled in the way these fools shrank away from him, but he kept this glee locked deep inside, showing them only the grim look of righteous anger. 'I was afraid he was up to somethin' like this when he give me the slip a coupla miles out of town.'

Haskins got the bullet out of the man's groin and looked up, wiping his bloody hands on a bar towel. But not until he had finished, until he had the man taken care of, did Doc open his mouth. What he asked then was a question. He looked McCartrey square in the eye.

'You claiming he done this?'

'You know any other cut-an'-runner around here?'

'Understand you quit that outfit. If so, how come...'

'I was bringin' him in. Just about spent the whole day gettin' him up to...'

'If that's the case, what was he doing with a gun on him?'

'I never took his hogleg.' McCartrey showed them a wintry grin. 'I was leavin' that up to you town jakes. I had the bastard all set to give you the... Hell! it was Fick shoved Clell at the parson.'

McCartrey pulled his shoulders together. 'Fick was bound an' determined the guy was a snoop sent in here to dig up the grief on them homesteaders. The ones Fick run out. But the thing I had Horner talked into spillin'—or thought I did—was the deal Fick give him to gun old man Fardel.'

'Your story and Clell's don't match. According to Clell *you* was going to do that. Same way,' Haskins said, 'you took care of that homesteader.'

McCartrey grinned. 'That Clell,' he said, chuckling, and shrugged.

'He also claimed you went out to Straddlebug. Said you jawed Fick into a stroke and, whiles he was passed out, set fire to the place.'

'You believe a thing like that?' McCartrey's expression made it evident to all that, so far as he was concerned, Doc could make it too crazy without lifting a foot. 'God almighty!' he said, and stamped out of there.

On the porch he swung around, hearing bootsteps coming after him. It was the other Boxed O puncher. 'Where you reckon,' this one said, 'that little bastard is now?'

'Don't come to me. I've plumb run out of doin' favors.'

'Hell, Mac. If you'd run into—'

'You guys're so smart, go ahead an' find

199

him.'

McCartrey picked up his reins and swung into the saddle. He still didn't know about Beaupre, but he reckoned he knew where to go to find out.

The night boss said, biting off a fresh chew, 'He was huntin' the parson. Parson went out to Crescent. You might try there.'

McCartrey flipped him a cartwheel and headed for the restaurant. He hadn't figured to put in another appearance at Fardel's until this thing was done with, but the more he cogitated the more convinced he became that, risk or no risk, he was going to have to do it. Beaupre, loose, could tie him in with those damned squatters. And where in hell was Horner?

He put down a good meal but his mind wasn't on it. He was reasonably sure he had this town bunch bluffed. Even if somebody took it on himself to ride out there and actually saw the gutted house, or even found Fick in the ashes, they couldn't bring it home to him. They had nothing but Clell's word and a dead horse packing his saddle. Haines would want more than that to move against a man like McCartrey. But if Beaupre squawked...

He dropped some change on the counter and stopped outside to build a smoke. If he could depend on that damned Kid... He scowled into the night and plumbed the depths of his frustrations. Horner'd had plenty of time to have done the job if he'd been going to.

He scratched the match in his fist, brought the flame to his face and, swearing, pitched the stick away from him.

*   *   *

Beaupre fell back as Irish stepped through the door and pulled it quietly shut behind him. Expecting trouble, the town man was braced for it, but not for the impact of the words Irish spoke. 'Fardel's dead. You can give me a hand with him.'

The saloon man's breath was a sound sharply sucked between bared teeth as Irish, catching his arm, steered him off through the gloom to where Fardel's horse stood restively pawing. Beaupre's arm flinched away as he pulled back from the bay's grisly burden.

'Not very pretty, is it?' Irish said grimly, and tersely sketched in the sequence of events which had preceded the Crescent owner's killing. 'Horner could have been laying there waiting for a target. The shot Fardel threw at that coyote could have fetched him. I rather think perhaps it did, and yet he must have been aware of the man we found in the grass or he'd have passed some words before shooting.'

'If he'd been waiting,' Beaupre nodded,

201

'he'd have taken that first shot at you. He's not the kind to forget...'

'Nor the kind to pass up a good chance at easy money,' Irish said flatly. 'What steps have you taken to keep his gun off you?'

Beaupre's shape turned still. For a long-drawn quarter of a minute it released no sound of breathing. Crickets scraped their wings. In the reeds along the shore a frog pushed out its throat and the shadows stirred near the back of the house. 'You're pretty sharp,' Beaupre said, 'for a preacher.'

'You're in this up to your neck, my friend. You've been conspiring with McCartrey to steal this range, helping him bankrupt Straddlebug and shaping Fick up for the goat when the crash comes. I'm sharp enough to know when you pulled Clell off my neck you weren't investing in the services of a preacher.'

Beaupre said thinly, 'I made no mistake about you.'

'Don't bank on that. You figured to throw me at McCartrey and come out with the lion's share. But McCartrey's got to have a range war if he's to throw enough dust to take over.'

'And you don't think...'

'I don't think he'll have the time. The Pima County sheriff has thrown a ring around this Basin. He's armed a bunch of Papago Indians and called in help from outside counties. McCartrey's waited too long to build his fire under Fick.'

You could tell by Beaupre's silence how much Irish's words had jolted him.

But they hadn't convinced him. Beaupre said, 'That posse's hunting for you. Haines won't move in this business; he'll straddle the fence until he sees how the wind blows. And after you've dealt with McCartrey, mister...'

'Maybe I won't be dealing with McCartrey.'

Beaupre laughed softly. 'You can't help yourself. He thinks you're a marshal. You'll get rid of him for me or he'll get rid of you.'

The silence piled up and ten feet behind them a spur rowel chimed against stone and Irish's jerked-around stare saw Primero's shape come out of the blackness. 'I go now,' the Mexican said.

'Who's this?' That was Beaupre.

Irish introduced them, neither man acknowledging it. Irish said to the saloon man, 'Regardless of anything else that might happen, Primero is Crescent's insurance.'

The town man, not understanding, shrugged indifferently. Irish caught the glint of the Mexican's teeth. As Primero, turning away, began to blend into the shadows, Irish said, 'We'd better keep Fardel here. We'll lay him out—'

'Just a minute.' Beaupre, staring after the

Mexican, growled: 'Where's that fellow off to?'

'Don't you think the coroner and Haines—'

'You damn fool!' Beaupre snarled, grabbing hold of him.

'Better take another look at your hole card.'

Beaupre shoved him away, shaking a gun from his sleeve. But Irish, expecting him to make this attempt, caught his wrist with a clamp of fingers, swung him round and wrenched the arm up behind him. The derringer, when Beaupre let loose of it, Irish dropped into his own left coat pocket. He let go of the man then. 'I think we've had all the shooting we need here.'

Beaupre, rubbing his wrist, kept his mouth shut. But he didn't need to speak for Irish to sense his animosity. The deadly aroma of it filled the night between them and Irish watched him closely until Primero rode past them and, beyond the yard, broke into a lope. He stepped over to the bay then, reaching for the knots. 'We'd better get Fardel into the house.'

He was loosening the rope when the saloon man lunged for his own mount. Irish's thumb clicked back the hammer of the derringer. 'I don't believe I'd try that, friend.'

Beaupre stopped in his tracks. He was

shaking with anger.

Irish, knowing the man's thoughts, could even sympathise a little, but his tone did not brook argument when he ordered Beaupre to help him. 'Take his feet,' Irish said, 'and lead the way. We'll take him round through the back. No—wait. We'll use the bunkhouse. Be a little easier on all of us, I reckon. Go ahead. And be careful.'

Beaupre, in front, was pushing open the door when Irish caught the sound of a wagon. 'Keep moving,' he said as Beaupre's head came about.

They put the body on a bunk. The town man distastefully wiped his hands on his pants legs. 'You're not through,' Irish said as Beaupre started for the door. 'There's a lamp on that table. Light it.'

He stood watching as the lamp's lambent flow spread across the silent room. 'Get his clothes off now and start washing him.'

Beaupre's stare was filled with outrage. His cheeks looked green and rebellion showed his temper in each stiff angle of his shape.

'Didn't imagine you were so finicky,' Irish said, producing the derringer.

He allowed the saloon man opportunity to have a good look down its muzzle. 'Puny-looking, isn't it? Young rattlers look pretty puny too and are just about as deadly when a man's standing as near as you are.'

Beaupre, swearing, turned back to the bunk. 'Never mind looking for his pistol,' Irish said; 'you'd be wasting your time.' After watching the man through a moment of silence he said, faintly smiling, 'I'm going to get his Sunday suit. What you do with your life is your own business, Beaupre, but if you value your health you'll stay right where you are.'

CHAPTER EIGHTEEN

The ungreased wheels of the rumbling wagon were rolling into the yard as Irish stepped outside. Through the inconstant shadows he could make out the flapping canvas of its Conestoga rigging, the humpy shapes of plodding oxen. He could not see the driver, but memory painted him into this picture as he'd been that night in town when Irish, bound for the hills, had glimpsed him peddling his bottled cure-all. The snake-oil quack—*Guaranteed to relieve every pain in your body!*

Irish, snorting, went round to the back as he had gone this morning, pulling open the screen, crossing the groaning boards of the porch and stepping into the lamplit kitchen. There was no one in sight, but Cherry's voice came faintly from beyond a closed

206

door; and he wondered what had become of Mrs Fardel. He reckoned someone ought to tell her, but didn't see why he should be that someone.

All his life, it seemed like, he had been pursued by the cares of others, put upon and burdened till he felt like that fellow in Coleridge's fantasy, the one with the bird hung around his neck. With Beaupre on tap and that bleach-eyed Kid somewhere sniffing his back trail... A man might make his bargains but only a dimwit made them rougher than he had to.

Still pulled two ways he moved past the sink, seeing the unwashed cups where Cherry had left them, frowning as Pauline again crept into the churn of his thinking. More and more disturbed, he had his brief wonder, and, knowing the folly of such thoughts, strode on up the hall, shutting her out of his mind. Trying to find some way through this dark plot of McCartrey's he came back to the Mexican, Primero.

The man was no fool. It might have been a mistake letting the fellow ride out of here, for there was no guarantee he would not stop in the town. The man might be a bandit, just as Irish believed, or some minor revolutionary holed up here for the moment, but he was also a Latin and therefore liable to act on impulse.

All a man could be sure of was that

Primero wanted Cherry and was convinced Irish also wanted her. It was against all logic that he would show his face in Red Post; but if he thought he might not get back in time to block Irish from running off with the girl he would be bound to take other measures. It was these 'other measures' Irish worried about. A visit from the law was the last thing Irish wanted right now. And there was Beaupre too to be reckoned with; he would not see all his hopes cut to doll-rags if he could find any way of preventing this. Once convinced he was whipped the man could be a mad dog.

Pauline, no longer in the rocker, was standing just inside the open front door, staring into the night. Beyond her Irish could see the dim shape of Cherry talking with someone at the edge of the veranda. Pauline turned, hearing Irish; and, observing the look in her wide-open eyes, he felt again that lift of inexplicable excitement she had stirred in him before.

The golden glow of the lamp built up the lustre of her hair, and this rich color warmed and softened the ivory pallor of her skin. There was a womanliness about her that touched and fired his senses powerfully, unsettling and disturbing the recent decisions he had made.

When she asked who it was, he said, 'No one to get upset about. Travelling quack with a medicine show. Probably looking for a...'

Cherry's heels tapped across the sagging planks of the veranda. 'He's here,' she said, 'come in if you want.' She moved into the light and across her shoulder Irish glimpsed the coonskin cap and grizzled hair of the man who followed her.

It was the snake-oil peddler. He paused inside the doorway, peeling off his roper's gloves. 'Gettin' blowy outside,' he said, brushing a hand across his bristles as he ducked a nod towards Pauline. It was the girl's stiffening look of astonishment that made Irish turn for another stare at the fellow.

*   *   *

Just short of dark on the fourteenth day Haines called off his manhunt. After all, this jamboree was being paid for by people who had put him in office, and, with another election coming on, he was too shrewd a campaigner to keep beating a dead dog. That gambler if he'd ever come into this country, must have had help to disappear so completely.

And where would he get it? There were plenty of shoestring spreads in these hills that had no love for a man packin' tin. Owlhooters likewise and a variety of lesser

209

cross-grained roughnecks who, for one reason or another, would give sustenance and hiding to a man on the dodge. It was at one such place, after sending home his Papagos, Haines stopped for a fresh mount, not yet having come to giving up his convictions entirely.

The sheriff's bitter eyes moved from the crowbait this man offered to the look of the man himself. The fellow told him, scowling, 'This horse will do just about anythin'.'

'He didn't say when he would do it, though, did he?'

As transportation it was the hardest riding bag of bones Haines had ever wrapped his legs about; and though he did not blame the nag, it was gall to have him throw a balk every time his eyes saw grass.

Haines finally gave up and cut back south. It was while he was on his way into town with night creeping darkly after him that he remembered the tight-lipped parson who had got off the stage in Red Post. He remembered other things then. The parson drowsing at his side but never with his mouth open, never rolling against him or snoring. And his elaborate confusion when he'd learned Red Post was the stop for the Basin. The way he'd helped the girl, and the look of him last night when they'd run into each other near Pilot Knob. His talk about Crescent and Straddlebug feuding, his obstinate insistence that Haines' quarry had fled north.

Of course he might have the right of that, but it was hard on Haines' pride to admit a mistake. 'To hell with him,' Haines snarled, jerking up the nag's head again. 'Get a move on, goddam it—don't petrify here!'

It was less than four hours to daylight when the irate lawman bucked the wind into town. Since he found the Ophir not yet locked up he took on a bait of grub before leading the borrowed horse to the livery, where he exchanged it for one of more serviceable build.

He swore as he thought of the long ride still ahead of him. But he had to get back; there was that case coming up and the judge would raise the rafters ... He scowled across at the dark hotel, thinking longingly of bed. But he was the kind of pelican who, once having put his hand to a thing, purely hated to abandon it; and surprised at finding light in the local sanctum of the law, cut across to the jail and, getting down, groaned into the office.

Jim Vaguely, Red Post's town marshal, looked up with an irritable scowl and then brightened. 'Thank God! Figured you'd still be out in the brush...'

'What's up?'

The marshal told him. All about the bad blood between Straddlebug and Crescent,

211

about the reported gunning of one of Fick's homesteaders laid by Clell onto McCartrey, who was no longer working for Fick, it appeared. He gave the whole of Clell's story for whatever it was worth and then moved onto the recent shooting in the Palace, winding up with McCartrey's appearance and comment.

'Where's McCartrey now?'

The town man shrugged. 'Got his horse an' rode off, that's all I can tell you.'

'You verify that fire at Straddlebug?'

'Not my business.'

'We'll remedy that,' Haines said, flipping a badge at him. 'You get out there on the double and find out what the score is. Anyone besides McCartrey seen Horner?'

The town law, frowning, shook his head. 'Not since that preacher backed him down last night.' Observing the sheriff's heightened interest, he enlarged a bit on it. 'Damnedest thing—'

'I'll talk with Beaupre. You get out to Fick's ranch.'

But Beaupre wasn't available, Haines discovered. When, like the dive-keeper, he got round to checking the livery and learned that Beaupre, hunting the parson, had headed for Crescent, his jaws clamped shut and he got on his horse like hell wouldn't have him.

Irish was too old a hand to let his face betray him. The man and his get-up had undergone considerable change, but Irish had listened too long to the pitch of that voice, observing too carefully this man's pale eyes, to be mistaken. This snake-oil faker was that same U.S. marshal who had sat beside Pauline on the stage coming up here. She had recognised him too.

The marshal said, 'How are you, Reverend? Looks like you been tangling with the hard end of someone's fists. I guess we all have to sometime.' He sighed and rasped his cheeks again. 'I've got a little problem I'd be glad to get your views on.' As Cherry turned away he scrinched his left eye in a wink. 'Being it's kind of personal, if the ladies will excuse us...' He got hold of Irish's elbow and deftly maneuvered him through the door.

They moved off the veranda and deeper into the churn of shadows. The wind was getting obstreperous, the rough edge of its guests smelling of dampness and greasewood and all the wild odors of life in the desert; and it came to Irish in the midst of his thinking how ironic and pervertedly reasonable it would be if, now Fardel was dead, the forsaken rains came.

And then he remembered it wasn't rain

McCartrey wanted; and so got back to himself, and recalled his father saying *The rough is only metal*, and let the hand he had been sliding towards his gun drop back to his side.

He would agree with that now in an abstract way, but the question was how to apply it. He felt himself sweating and there was a coldness in his belly that had nothing to do with this wind.

The marshal said, voice cautiously lowered, 'Where's Beaupre and what did he come out here for?'

Irish felt relief pounding through him, loosening up locked muscles; and rather irritably remembered his was not a marshal's case. Then suspicion tightened the giddiness out of him, for the law was just as corrupt as its servants and this man had come out here in a garb calculated to conceal his identity. They were two of a kind. *Two wolves in lambs' clothing.*

'He's in the bunkhouse,' Irish said, forcing himself to sound casual, and told him what the saloon man was doing and how Cherry's father had lost his life. 'In a way I feel responsible. If I hadn't insisted that Fardel go out there—'

'You're sure it was that fellow Horner that shot him?'

'It was the Kid, if that's who you mean. I'm not likely to forget him.' Irish mentioned

214

the run-in he had had with the man in town.

'Why'd you let Clell work you over?'

Irish pushed that around in his mind for a while with the cold spot growing in the pit of his belly. He was not concerned with revealing the truth but rather with the vistas the marshal's question opened up, confirming as it did the man's grim interest in Irish's movements. He couldn't find anything to throw in the way of that interest. Not even a good lie.

'This Beaupre,' the marshal went on as though never having considered the possibility of Irish answering, 'is a very sly duck; but feathers get singed when they're fetched too near to a fire. Which is a thing most folks aren't in the habit of giving much thought to, if you get what I mean. There's a lot of queer talk flying around about town, and some of it, I imagine, bellies up to the truth. Your friend Clell, by the way, got himself killed tonight.'

You're pretty cute too, Irish thought; and wondered how much rope the man was planning to give him.

'He had been running off of the jaw and it seems to have caught up with him,' the marshal said dryly, 'in Beaupre's bar.'

Again Irish felt the quick lift of respite, but he had made up his mind about this badge-packer now, and, staring through the blackness at that whisker-stubbed face, he

215

merely nodded his head.

The marshal turned a little in a natural impatience so that the strike of his stare had points of lamplight in it, picked up from the open door. 'I think we'll question—'

A shot rang out, oddly muted in the wind but unmistakably originating from somewhere about the bunkhouse; and the marshal whirled, breaking into a run, Irish pressing him so close he was thrown off-stride when the lawman stopped just outside the nearest window. There was nothing to be seen from here except the glint of the gun in the marshal's fist. Between gusts of the wind they caught the flutter of running feet and dashed round the building in fierce pursuit, the marshal panting.

But there was no one in sight, and when they stopped there was nothing to be heard beyond the whipped-up roughness of the wind. 'Be raining by morning,' the marshal growled. 'Which way'd he go?'

Irish, staring into the wind, pointed right. 'Behind that shed, I think. He won't get far that way.'

Pacing the lawman, bearing more to the west, stumbling once when he got hung up in some briers, Irish worked in closer, bending frequently in the hope of sighting their quarry should the marshal's advance force the man to shift location.

There was nothing in back of the shed but

black open for a good fifty yards until you came against the shale of the slope that climbed into timber where Irish, this morning, had gone with Cherry.

Ahead of Irish now and to the left of the shed was the network of corrals, and as he paused, a horse there snorted. Irish wanted to warn the marshal, but if he called he'd betray his own position. His searching hand found a rock and he lobbed it a little to the right of the point where the horse had been startled; and left of that place a gun exploded.

The marshal triggered three times. Wind whirled the sound away and there was nothing but blackness where the first gun had spoken. Far down to the left, near the end of the pens, something moved. A horse whinnied back of the house, and Irish, abandoning caution, broke out of his crouch and ran hard in that direction.

Someone had snuffed the kitchen lamp and the back of the house was completely without light when he came abreast the rear porch and stopped, trying to hear through the sound of his breathing. He swore when the wind brought a mutter of hoofbeats and the marshal swore too, coming out of the gloom. 'Let him go,' he growled, puffing.

'Any idea who it was?'

The marshal, without answering, struck off in silence towards the shine of the bunkhouse lamp.

'Parson?'

Irish, turning, looked into the solid gloom of the porch. The screen door skreaked. She came towards him swiftly, soundlessly barefoot. 'He's gone,' Irish said, 'whoever he was.' Cherry's hand found his arm, her fingers closing convulsively. 'I was afraid ...' She pushed against him, shivering.

Irish stood there stiffly, resisting the impulse to comfort her. Light sprang up in the kitchen. The porch took shape behind the gleam of her hair and he stepped back away from her as the bright rectangle of the inner door widened. He saw Pauline, partially blocking that light, lift a hand to shade her eyes.

Cherry chose that moment to come against him again. Going up on her toes she locked both arms about his neck, moulding herself to him, stubbornly clinging even after the closing door left them alone in the windy darkness.

She let him take her arms away then and laughed up at him softly. 'She won't want you now. All her life she has been first...'

CHAPTER NINETEEN

Irish was noticeably seething when he stepped inside the bunkhouse. Looking up, the marshal growled, 'Don't worry—we'll have that lad by the heels before long or my name ain't Jack Robinson.'

'You know who he was?'

'I know there wouldn't be many wanting Beaupre dead bad enough to gun him. Follows the same pattern as Clell's killing tonight in Red Post,' he explained, covering Beaupre. 'While that's not proof it rather narrows it down.'

Irish realized now why the man had asked if he were sure it was the Kid who'd shot Fardel. The scene of Fardel's killing was nearly eighteen miles from Red Post.

The marshal considered him blandly. 'What I'm trying to do is put each blame where it properly belongs. I can't believe these deaths are all the work of one man, though it's conceivable one man's behind them; and,' he said with a sudden tight smile, 'I haven't forgotten you.'

The walls of the room fled away from Bert Irish and the cry of the wind became a cold sound around him. He stood and stood, not moving, scarce blinking, while the coldness grew inside his bones.

He could feel the marshal's eyes leanly watching, trying to pick his thoughts apart. He could not judge how long the silence held but found himself staring at the blanketed men—at those two still shapes beyond the cold and the fear; and he heard himself say, 'Man's days are as grass. O God, forgive us our careless blundering...'

The marshal said briskly, 'Amen.'

Irish took a deep breath. 'We'd better get back to the ladies.'

'You go ahead. We were chasing a prowler. Don't mention what's happened to Beaupre; no use in alarming them more—' He broke off. 'Rain,' he said, and Irish heard the drops too. The marshal sighed. 'I think I'll move my rig around back of the barn and stay out of sight a while.'

'You think McCartrey...'

'One thing you learn in my line of work, Irish, is to pay no attention to what people say. Facts don't change. When I get enough facts there'll be no need of thinking.'

Irish!

*   *   *

Pauline, stiffly erect in the uncomfortable rocker, was regarding the hands in her lap when Cherry, padding in from out back, said bluntly: 'Now you know what it's like to want something you can't have.'

Pauline, continuing to stare at her fingers, neither moved nor answered. Cherry, angered, said fiercely, 'He would always come back to me—you know he would!'

Pauline, her look agitated, got up and crossed to the window. 'It's raining,' she said, sounding surprised, after a moment.

'Is that all you can say?'

Pauline's silence remained unbroken.

'Why don't you face up to it?' Cherry cried bitterly. 'I know why you came here. It'll do you no good! He—'

There was a clatter out back. The porch screen slammed. The parson came in, shaking the wet off his coat, looking first at Pauline, then at Cherry and back again. 'What's up?'

Pauline, turning away from the window, met Irish's glance straightly. Cherry caught hold of his arm, but his eyes continued to search Pauline; and they were that way, caught up in their black thinking, when McCartrey, dripping trails of glistening water, came tramping in off the veranda and heeled the door shut back of him.

Water beaded the black brush of his cavalry mustache and dripped off his chin and off the point of his hat as his cold eyes studied Irish through a moment of vacuum while wind rushed rain across the yard and slatted the windows like a gout from a hose. McCartrey loosened his slicker with a twist of broad shoulders and spoke to the pale-cheeked girl by the wall. 'A fine chase you've led me! Get a blanket from Cherry and let's be on our way.'

'No,' Pauline said. 'I'll go nowhere with you.'

The Straddlebug man looked fed up with her tantrums. 'You'll go. You'll go if—'

'You heard her, McCartrey.'

The man's head came around. He seemed surprised, thinly amused. 'Who's this?' he said, and stepped back for a longer, sharper look, forcing Irish to wheel half round to keep track of him. The black glistening shine of the rain-wet window showed now on McCartrey's left. Irish glimpsed his own reflection starkly mirrored against things behind him.

'Parson,' Cherry said; and McCartrey's look, whipped contemptuously away from him, skewered Pauline. 'Your dad's had a stroke. Doc don't hold out much chance for him. You figure to see him before he goes you sure as hell better move lively.'

Pauline's staring eyes looked too big for her face.

McCartrey said, 'You goin' or ain't you?'

She didn't want to believe him but was plainly afraid not to.

Irish said, 'I think the man's lying,' and saw the sharp hole suddenly appear in the glass as something cuffed at his coat and

222

slammed into the wall. Cherry screamed through the muted sound of the gun and outside someone shouted. McCartrey, firing wildly into the night, caught the lamp off the table and snuffed it. Irish shifted away from where he had stood. Damp wind laced with rain came through the smashed window and Irish ducked as the lamp sailed past his head.

Spurred boots rushed across the floor, moving away from him. Somewhere back of him Cherry was whimpering, and Pauline, near the window, cried out and went even more suddenly still.

Through the gun smell and racket Irish glimpsed struggling shapes bearing down on the door and flung himself that way, forgetting he was armed—forgetting everything except that McCartrey, plainly desperate, was attempting to take Pauline with him.

Irish's fist found McCartrey's head. The man's hands fell away from the girl and she spun clear of him, jerking open the door and stumbling through it. Coming half around, McCartrey pushed himself off the wall. Before he could get set Irish was into him again, lashing out with both fists, wild to beat the man insensible. The very fury of this attack created the chance McCartrey needed. Suddenly twisting, McCartrey lunged, belting Irish across the chest with his pistol.

It very nearly floored him.

McCartrey, had he pressed his advantage, might have ended it then. He must have been obsessed with the loss of the girl. Scarcely able to breathe Irish floundered after him, catching the tail of the slicker as McCartrey ducked through the door. The man tried to shake him off, to get out of the thing, but couldn't get enough slack. He whirled then, cursing, trying to beat Irish's head with the pistol. He overreached, and Irish, closing, wrapped both arms about his middle. They went down, Irish losing his hold.

McCartrey was up soonest but got a spur hooked into his slicker. While he was trying to free it Irish rolled into the other leg, tripping him. He spilled heavily onto the rain-slick planks and the gun went skittering out of his hand.

Match flame ravelled through the blackness of the house, and Cherry, finding another lamp, came hurrying towards them. Light rushed through the open door, and Irish, wheezing, clambered onto his feet in time to dodge McCartrey's boot. He kicked McCartrey's other leg out from under him, and when the man got up knocked him down again. His hat rolled off, but McCartrey was tough. He lurched onto his feet and, half crouching, swung, this blow sending Irish crashing into the wall.

The salty stickiness of blood dribbled into Irish's mouth. He scrubbed the back of a hand across smashed lips and glimpsed Pauline's shocked face staring out of the dripping shadows. Something clattered in the bunkhouse across the yard, and McCartrey, wild to get away now, came slashing in with swinging fists. Irish, trying to trade blows, was hampered by the wall and took considerable punishment. Shaking his head to give his eyes focus he found McCartrey measuring him, cocking his balance to end this. McCartrey's arm drew back.

Irish ducked and, using the wall's leverage, came up inside the hurtling swing of that arm, connecting solidly with McCartrey's jaw. McCartrey went through the rickety railing.

He got up slowly, half in light, half out of it, and seemed to be having trouble with his back. He paid no attention to Irish's stumbling approach, but when Irish reached to catch hold of his shoulder he came out of his crouch with a wicked grin. 'Sucker!' he jeered; and Irish, caught flatfooted, saw the glint of a knife.

'You got a gun under your arm,' McCartrey mocked, 'drag it.'

Bert Irish knew he could never get hold of it. Time had finally abandoned him, and in that moment of enormous astonishment he suddenly realized what he had been doing here—that he had forgotten to be afraid. Cold sweat came into the palms of his hands and he could feel the fear creeping up through his legs. He fought for control with all the will there was in him, swallowing the sourness that came out of his stomach, knowing he was too close to the man even to reach Beaupre's pocketed derringer before the bright steel of that blade ripped into him. But he was tensing to try when Pauline said, 'Bates, let go of the knife.'

McCartrey laughed, his eyes watching Irish with a cold relish now. 'Sure hate to disappoint you, baby. That gun you picked up is empty—'

'This one's not,' the marshal's voice said out of the drizzling gloom. 'It's in the hand of a U.S. marshal and I'd advise you to do what the lady told you.'

Irish correctly read the glittering look that came into the range boss's gone-still stare. The hand gripping the knife was concealed from the marshal by McCartrey's burly shape, and even as the man shrugged the dejected slump of broad shoulders Irish knew he was fixing to whirl and throw that blade.

He did the only thing he could think of. Stumbling into the man Irish carried him off balance, pounding him with short-arm jabs wherever he was lucky enough to make contact, staggering around with McCartrey in a kind of drunken frolic while putting everything he had into keeping that knife away from him. It was nerve-breaking, breath-taking, terrible work, for the man, now frantic, had the strength of desperation.

Irish knew that sweat-slippery wrist was twisting out of his control when without warning McCartrey's legs shot from under him, dropping them both in a snarling tangle of struggling limbs. It was Irish's bad luck to be caught underneath and on the rain-slick gumbo of that puddled adobe he could get no purchase to lever himself over. Many things passed through the mill of his mind in the moment McCartrey's knife hand got away from him. But he felt no fear, only a kind of sad regret that a wasted life should have to end like this, yet it was ironically fitting that he should die in the mud. Die with lips still locked over the things that in some better circumstances he would have said to Pauline Fick.

He knew the knife was coming down and tried in vain to twist aside. His spurless heels could find no purchase; then McCartrey, on top of him, went suddenly limp.

Irish felt as though he might have lost track of time some place. He could remember no gunshot. Pushing McCartrey away he got painfully up to find the marshal beside him. The marshal's head was turned listening; the squelchy sound of nearing hoofs came grayly out of the curtain of rain. He saw Pauline too, and in the house he could hear Cherry talking to her mother.

The lamps golden light no longer came from the door, yet he could see Pauline quite well. She was watching the marshal; and Irish considering both of them, realized the night was gone. Glancing down at his soaking mud-stained clothes he forced all expression off his face. This was the time—that inevitable day—which he had known all along must eventually catch up with him.

He heard Pauline asking, 'What are you going to do?'

The marshal looked at her and grinned. Something passed between those two but Irish could make nothing of it. 'McCartrey's the jigger I'm after.' The lawman swivelled his glance at Irish. 'I'll take that gun you've got under your arm. And that hide-out you've got in your pocket.'

Irish handed them over. He wasn't kidding himself.

The horseman came up through the drizzle, staring curiously. It was no one Irish had encountered before, but the man was apparently known to the others; his horse had the Straddlebug brand on its hip. 'Chunks,' said the marshal, 'what's on your mind this fine morning?'

Though Irish did not know him, this was the man Pauline had heard her father bawl out for running his horse so hard in the heat. He touched his hat to the girl but spoke to the marshal. 'We had a fire out there. Fick's dead,' he said, staring down at McCartrey, who was beginning to come round, 'What happened to his face?'

Pauline turned away, walking blindly towards the house. Through the rain Irish watched her with his gray thoughts unwinding in the bleakness of self-knowledge.

The marshal looked at McCartrey. 'I had to bat him a couple of times with my gun barrel.' They watched the man squirm over and sit up with a deal of groaning. 'Anything else out there I should know about?'

'Was some talk for a while about levellin' this place, but, lackin' the push this galoot would of give 'em, it kind of run out like some of his hardcases. No one there now but what's left of the crew. And a dead bronc in the yard with McCartrey's gear on 'im. I had 'em leave it alone, figured you might want to see it.'

McCartrey took bloody hands away from his face. 'That saddle was stole. I ain't been near the damn place since that old bastard told—'

'Mebbe,' Chunks grinned, 'you'd like to hear what he told me. He'd managed to roll off the porch. He wasn't dead when I got to him—'

'Lies!' McCartrey sneered. 'You'll have a time gettin' anyone to believe—'

'I'll take Chunks' word,' the marshal said. 'I think a jury'll take it too. You didn't know it when you hired him, but Chunks is one of my deputies. What did Fick have to say?'

'Said McCartrey was out there. Said he smashed a lit lantern and burned the place up deliberate. That the idea of gettin' rid of them homesteaders was hatched an' carried out by—'

'Lies!' McCartrey surged to his feet, but broke off in a spate of cursing when the marshal levelled the 'Peacemaker' with which he had prevented the man from putting the knife into Irish.

'Chunks,' he said, 'fetch a rope while I humor him.'

Irish thought the marshal's term largely exaggerated under the circumstances. When the rope was brought and McCartrey trussed to the officer's satisfaction, Irish was asked to help the man into the house. 'We'll be on our way,' Chunks was told, 'very shortly. I think the ladies are due a few words of explanation and it would hardly be seemly to ask them—'

'I need a doctor,' McCartrey growled, glowering.

'You need have no concern,' the marshal

230

said; 'you'll get everything that's coming to you. Meantime, Chunks, you can be catching up some horses. We'll need ... Let me see—we'll need about six, counting Beaupre and Horner. Take the best you can find, for we shall want to move spryly.' He sleeved the rain off his face and readjusted his hat brim. 'Now, gentlemen, if you'll precede me ...'

* * *

The two girls moved back from the door as they tramped in. The lamp McCartrey had grabbed off the table had been replaced by another whose wick was turned high to combat the day's gloom. The girls had evidently come to some kind of truce, for they remained close together. Pauline had changed her wet clothes for some patched things of Cherry's, which, though plainly too tight, certainly enhanced her appearance. Beyond that first look Irish kept his eyes off her.

The marshal said briskly, 'I thought you ladies might like to know that all the trouble around here is over. There will naturally be a few changes ...'

Irish thought of Primero; and his mind, still trying to find a way out of this, took hope—even though his judgment scornfully told him this was preposterous. The border was almost thirty miles away and even after the Mexican crossed it he would not find the help he had gone for by snapping his fingers. His friends would have to be gathered...

'And so you can see,' the marshal was saying, 'everything that has happened has been the work of one man, Bates McCartrey; not altogether directly, of course, but all of it caused by wheels his activities put into motion. Ambition, within reason, is admirable. But when it gets out of hand and becomes an obsession—'

'You'll have a hell of a time pinning that on me in front of a jury,' McCartrey scoffed, but the marshal smiled imperturbably.

'Some of it perhaps, but we will prove enough to hang you. I've talked to some of those homesteaders and Chunks has talked to some of your crew. We may not be able to pin all of it on you, but I think Fick's death and Beaupre's certainly—'

'All you've got is a bunch of wild ideas!'

'I've got the Kid and I've got his statement. He will claim you hired him to kill Beaupre and Irish and he's got the cash in his pocket to prove it. Before I get done I'll have a witness in town who can place you behind that smashed window at the Palace with a gun in your hand while Clell was being killed. In Beaupre's safe we'll find a deposition in Beaupre's own hand that will tie you in with what happened to those homesteaders. I think you will discover we have enough to take care of you.'

When McCartrey ran out of wind Irish caught the same sound that sent Cherry across the room to pull open the front door. They all heard it then. Cherry, looking fed up, said, 'If this keeps up we'll have the whole town out here!'

Irish, still thinking of Primero, knew the uselessness of hoping. The Mexican had no love for him. It wasn't Primero anyway; he understood that when the boots struck the steps, came slogging across the wet planks of the veranda. When he saw Haines' leathery face in the door he let go of his breath and squared tired shoulders.

The sheriff, gun in hand, came at once to the point. 'I want you, Irish—'

'He's already under arrest,' the marshal said. 'He gave up his guns.'

'What's he doin' with his hands loose?'

'He's been helping me corral your friend McCartrey.'

'Pat,' McCartrey snarled, 'tell this damn fool...'

The sheriff had a one-track mind. Paying no attention to the ex-Straddlebug ramrod, he said to the marshal belligerently, 'I'll take care of Irish!' and slipped a pair of handcuffs out of his hip pocket.

'Your privilege,' the marshal smiled.

Irish said, 'Sheriff, I've got a money-belt

around me I'd be obliged if you would give Cherry Fardel over there. For your mother,' he told the girl. 'To take care of her after you and Tony get hitched.'

Haines got the belt and gave it to her. Irish didn't see the look of her at that moment. His glance was locked with Pauline's, and what he saw made the thought of where he was going now intolerable. Yet it gave him the courage to face it and he moved ahead of Haines towards the door with his chin up.

'He'll be back,' the marshal said to Pauline. 'You may depend on that. You've got my word for it.'

Nelson Nye was born in Chicago, Illinois. He was educated in schools in Ohio and Massachusetts and attended the Cincinnati Art Academy. His early journalism experience was writing publicity releases and book reviews for the *Cincinnati Times-Star* and the *Buffalo Evening News*. In 1935 he began working as a ranch hand in Texas and California and became an expert on breeding quarter horses on his own ranch outside Tucson, Arizona. Much of this love for horses can be found in exceptional novels such as WILD HORSE SHORTY and BLOOD OF KINGS. He published his first Western short story in THRILLING WESTERN and his first Western novel in 1936. He continued from then on to write prolifically, both under his own name and the bylines Drake C. Denver and Clem Colt. During the Second World War, he served with the U.S. Army Field Artillery. In 1949–1952 he worked as horse editor for TEXAS LIVESTOCK JOURNAL. He was one of the founding members of the Western Writers of America in 1953 and served twice as its president. His first Golden Spur Award from the Western Writers of America came to him for best Western reviewer and critic in 1954. In 1958–1962 he was frontier fiction reviewer for the *New York Times Book Review*. His second Golden Spur came for his novel LONG RUN. His virtues as an author of Western fiction include a tremendous sense of authenticity, an ability to keep the pace of a story from ever lagging, and a fecund inventiveness for plot twists and situations. Some of his finest novels have had off-trail protagonists such as THE BARBER OF TUBAC and both NOT GRASS ALONE and STRAWBERRY ROAN are notable for their outstanding female characters. His books have sold over 50,000,000 copies worldwide and have been translated into the principal European languages. The *Los Angeles Times* once praised him for his 'marvelous lingo, salty humor, and real characters.' Above all, a Nye Western possesses a vital energy that is both propulsive and persuasive.